MYSTERY AT THE JHC RANCH

W. C. Tuttle

Curley Publishing, Inc.
South Yarmouth, Ma.

Library of Congress Cataloging-in-Publication Data

Tuttle, W. C. (Wilbur C.)
  Mystery at the JHC Ranch / W. C. Tuttle.
    p. cm.
  Large print ed.
  1. Large type books. I. Title.
  [PS3539.U988M8 1990]
  813'.52—dc20
  ISBN 0–7927–0637–4 (hardcover)   90–36916
  ISBN 0–7927–0638–2 (softcover)   CIP

Copyright © 1932 by Houghton Mifflin & Company

Published in Large Print by arrangement with Donald MacCampbell, Inc. in the United States, Canada, the U.K. and British Commonwealth and the rest of the world market.

Distributed in Great Britain, Ireland and the Commonwealth by CHIVERS LIBRARY SERVICES LIMITED, Bath BA1 3HB, England.

Printed in Great Britain

MYSTERY AT THE JHC RANCH

Mystery at the JHC Ranch
CHAPTER I

'It shore was a funny thing when yuh come to think about it. Here was me and Jim Gavin on 'joinin' ranches, line fences so close together that the posts rubbed each other for a mile or more. There was sort of a hump, and up on that hump was Jim's big spring, flowin' plenty water to handle all his cows.

'Below the hump, on my land, was jist a trickle. It wasn't hardly enough for one cow a day. Been thataway ever since I knew the place. Well, sir, one day me and a couple of the boys decides to dig out that trickle and see if we can't get enough water to do us a little good. Know what it done? Well, sir, it must 'a' tapped that spring, 'cause we got all the water, and Jim never got deep enough to stop it. There was a granite wall runnin' deep into the earth, which must 'a' dammed it up, forcin' the water up to Jim's big spring.

'And that started all the trouble. Water down there is worth its weight in somethin' more valuable than gold. Yuh can't estimate what she's worth. The J Bar 44 shore went high and handsome. Gavin aimed to sue me, but the lawyer showed him where he was wrong. Then the J Bar 44 went on the warpath. There was shore a handful of Gavins and only one of me. I didn't want to drag my men into a killin'.

'Me and Jim Gavin meets in town, and he throwed down on me, after a few words was said, but I beat him to the draw and I shore tombstoned that jigger. It was a even break and the law didn't do anythin', but I knowed it was plenty war in the sack for me; so I came here to Los. Me, I'm an old man, sixty-nine m' last birthday. I ain't goin' back there. It's been two years, but Gavins don't forgit nothin' in two years.'

The speaker was a little old man, whose thin face bore leather-like wrinkles, worn deep by sun and sand, a scraggly gray mustache, heavy brows, and a square chin. He lounged back in a rocking-chair, his sock-clad feet on a tapestry-covered stool, and smoked a home-made cigarette. He wore no coat or vest, and his collar was minus a top button.

Seated at a little table was the only other occupant of the little apartment living-room, a man of about thirty years of age, black-haired, swarthy, immaculate of dress, his small mustache waxed sharply above a thin-lipped mouth. His nose was thin and sharp,

2

his dark eyes habitually gloomy.

On the table at his elbow was an open brief-case of stamped leather, and before him on the table were several sheets of paper. He tapped nervously on the table with a gold pencil, as the old man talked in the vernacular of the rangeland. He selected a cigarette from a thin silver case.

'I never heard before why you left there,' he said.

'That's kinda funny, Hal. Yore brother knowed all about it. Why, he was there in the saloon at the time. He's c'nected with the bank there, ain't he? Told me he was closin' up his assay office. Not much doin' there in that line. How I know about the bank stuff – he wrote me a while back, makin' me a offer for my ranch. Not me, I'll tell yuh. Not that I've got anythin' ag'in' any of the bank folks, but I've got a hunch that the Gavin outfit wants my ranch. I'll see 'em in hell up to the eyebrows first.'

'Did they make you a good offer, Mr. Cleland?'

'Shore! Too dam' good. But I don't have to sell. I reckon you know it now.'

Harold Welden, young attorney-at-law, nodded slowly, as he glanced at the penciled notes on his papers. There was no doubt that 'Million Dollar' Cleland was financially able

3

to live out the rest of his life in comfort, even without any revenue from his Arizona cattle ranch.

'The thing f'r you to do,' continued Cleland, blowing a stream of smoke toward the ceiling, 'is to marry Clare Nolan. Yeah, I know you've been shinin' around her considerable. Didn't know she'd be well fixed when I kicked out, eh?'

The old man chuckled softly, his eyes on the ceiling.

'She don't know it either. I like to surprise folks. I shore surprised old Jim Gavin. Thought I'd forgot how to draw and shoot. Clare ain't no kin of mine. Damn it, I ain't got no kin. Two days after I got here, a street car hit me kerplunk and busted m' off laig. Clare was the first one to git to me. She got the ambylance, and she went to the hospital with me.

'I thought she was a female doctor, and I cussed like hell, 'cause I never believed in wimmin doctors. She found out where I lived, and it was jist across the street from her. She got me a Chink boy to take care of the house, after I got moved out there, and every mornin' and evenin' she'd come over and talk with me. Read stories t' me, and wrote letters f'r me. I never was no hand f'r a pencil.

'By golly, she took care of me, jist as

4

though I was handsome. 'S a fact. Bein' a clerk in a office, she didn't have a lotta time, but she shore was good to me. I never told her I had money. Sometimes I hinted that I was havin' a tough time gittin' along, and she offered to lend me money. Can yuh match that? You marry her, young man; she's too dam' good for yuh, but she's too good f'r any man, as far as that goes.'

Welden's gloomy eyes shifted from contemplation of his papers, and his brows drew down in a scowl as he replied:

'I asked her to marry me – before I came here tonight.'

'Yuh did? You – huh! Turned yuh down, eh?'

Welden took a deep breath and his lips tightened.

'She said I drank and gambled too much.'

'Ye-a-ah? Well, yuh do, don't yuh?'

Welden eyed the old man coldly. 'How did she know that?'

The old man squinted thoughtfully, gnawing at a wisp of his mustache.

'Mebby,' he said slowly, 'she's in communication with a little bird.'

Welden snorted angrily. He had a deep suspicion that J. H. 'Million Dollar' Cleland was the little bird.

'Yuh *do* drink too much, Hal, and yuh run

with a lotta wild ones. No woman wants a whiskey soak, nor she don't want a gambler. They ain't dependable. No, I don't blame her for turnin' yuh down. Shows good sense.'

The lawyer picked up his papers and put them in his brief-case.

'You fix up that will,' said the old man. 'Put in everythin' I've said, and make one provision pretty prominent.'

'Which one is that?'

'The one where I say she can't never sell the JHC. I shore want that understood, 'cause the Gavins will be after her to sell.'

'Rather a foolish provision.'

'Foolish – hell! It's my ranch until I die, and I'll give it away with all m' ropes tied to it. Clare will understand. And – well, you write it out, and I'll show it to a dozen lawyers, before I sign it. There ain't goin' to be no holes in that legal fence. She'll be horse-high, bull-strong, and sheep-tight. Ain't nobody goin' to shoot *my* will full of holes.'

Welden nodded, a rather sarcastic smile on his thin lips.

'Rather doubting my ability to make it foolproof, eh?'

'Wantin' to be sure of it, Hal. No, I ain't doubtin' yuh. I've knowed yuh a long time, and yore brother and me was friends, but I'm only goin' t' die once, and only goin' to give away my property once; so I'm shore goin' to see everythin' made up right.'

'You'll prob'ly outlive a lot of us yet.'

'Prob'ly – but the odds are ag'in me. You lemme know when it's fixed.'

'I'll bring it up to you in a rough draft, and we'll go over it together.'

'That's the stuff. Have a little snifter of whiskey before yuh go?'

'No!' shortly.

'Well, I'll have to go alone, then. I ain't in love, and I'm too danged old to do anythin' foolish; so I reckon it's safe.'

They shook hands, and the lawyer went out. The old man produced a bottle of liquor from a little cabinet, and drank a generous hooker straight. He grimaced, grinned to himself, and then yawned widely. His apartment was on the ground floor on a palm-lined street, removed from the heavy traffic. There was a small stretch of lawn, with flowers, and flowering shrubbery, wafting their perfume through his open front window on a breeze from the Pacific.

He walked over to the window and drew the curtain aside, drinking in a deep breath of the fresh air. Farther up the street, the huge globe of a street-lamp looked like a full moon through the palm fronds. As far

7

as any sound was concerned, he might have been miles away from a city.

Across the street was another two-story apartment, and he could see a light up in Clare's room. Clare was a queer girl, he thought. Not like any other girl he had ever known. So unselfish that she was willing to give up her time to amuse and comfort an old man. Clare was an orphan, whose parents had been killed in a big fire. She had told him quite a lot about them.

But he had told her nothing about himself, except that he was from Arizona. It was true he had told her stories of the cattle country, but he did not figure in any of them. She didn't ask questions. Her salary was not large, but was ample for her needs, it seemed to him. He had thought of trying to give her some money, but knew she wouldn't accept.

Now he had instructed Welden to make out that will, leaving everything he owned to Clare. She would never have to work again. He smiled to himself, trying to visualize her, when the will was read. In spite of his years, he was as active and wiry as a young man, but something had prompted him to make this will. He didn't know what it was. Perhaps it was what he termed a 'hunch.'

In case he died intestate, the court would be obliged to handle the matter, and he was afraid of the Gavin family. It was sort of an obsession with him – the fear that those Gavins would get his ranch. As he stood there, leaning against the side of that large window, with the perfume of the flowers in his nostrils, his mind wandered back to that day in Cinco City. He was standing with his back against the Chuck Wagon Saloon bar, when Jim Gavin came in alone.

Gavin was a huge man, with a square jaw, flat cheek-bones, his black hair growing down the back of his neck, like the roach on a bear. His voice was a roar, even in ordinary conversation. He had stopped short, his eyes narrowing, at sight of Cleland.

'Yuh dam' water thief!' he snorted. 'I've been lookin' for you.'

'I ain't been away,' Cleland had answered.

'No, yuh ain't, but yo're goin'. I'll make this country too hot to hold yuh, Cleland.'

'Not you alone, Gavin.'

'Yeah – and right now!'

Gavin's huge right hand snapped back to his holster, and he ripped out his big Colt. But his draw was too late. Cleland's lips were drawn back, as he looked out across the little apartment-house lawn, and his right hand swayed back along his thigh, where there was no holstered gun now.

And just then something struck him a heavy

9

blow on the chest, as he heard the ringing report of a revolver shot. It hurt him – that heavy blow. He was unable to breathe, as he staggered back, dimly wondering, wondering. No, Jim Gavin didn't hit him. He had dropped Gavin. Where was he? The objects in the room were going around and around. Queer acting things, he thought. He was going down now, and he flung out his hand to save himself.

He didn't feel the crash of the fall, because the pain in his chest was too great. But he must be on the floor. He could see better now. Directly above his head was a light. He got up on one elbow, his brain whirling. In that position he felt a little easier and he tried to examine his chest. It was all sticky with blood. Funny, he thought. Gavin didn't shoot him. His brain cleared, and he realized that someone had shot him through the window.

He knew he was badly hurt. Someone went running past, pounding heavily on the pavement. Probably a policeman, who had heard the shot. Cleland wanted to call to him, but he had no voice. He tried to shift his position, and his elbow struck something. It was the table, which he had overturned in his fall.

'Must 'a' upset things,' he said to himself. Two people were talking out there in the street, but he couldn't hear what they were saying.

His brain was very clear now. The carpet was getting a good soaking of blood, but he didn't care much.

'Gavin,' he said to himself. 'One of 'em sneaked in on me. They want the ranch, but they won't get it. Clare'll get it.'

Then came a terrifying thought. Suppose he did not live long enough to sign that will? It would be of no value without his signature. He gritted his teeth against the pain, and tried to get up, but it was no use.

'They've got me whipped,' he told himself. 'Got me whipped, damn 'em! They laid for me, and they –'

His eyes blinked queerly. Within reach of him was a bottle of ink, which had fallen off the table, and the pen was sticking near it, point in the carpet. Under a corner of the table was a sheet of paper, which Welden had not used and had forgotten. Like a man in a haze, Cleland secured the pen, opened the bottle of ink, and tore the sheet of paper in getting it loose.

He was getting very weak, but his weakness only made him more determined to beat the Gavin gang. With an unsteady hand he dated the note, and wrote with many a blot,

11

smearing the bottom of the sheet with his own blood.

This is my last will, so help me God, and I no what I am doing when I give everything I own to Clare Nolan. I mean everythin' encluding the JHC ranch and everything on it near Cinco City, Arizona, but she can't never sell it to nobody. She don't need to go to no law about this cause shes smart enough to handle it herself.

Yours truly
John Henry Cleland
knowed as Million Dollar.
PS I no who shot me.

At the end of the postscript was a splatter of ink, where the broken pen went through the paper and snapped off short, and the penholder was still gripped in Cleland's fingers when the police examined the body, after they were notified by a thoroughly frightened Chinese boy, who had been out that evening and had come home about midnight.

The policeman on that beat had heard the shot. The landlady of the apartment had heard it, but thought it was the back-fire from a truck. She was rather grief-stricken over it all. Cleland had been a good tenant.

'Any close friends?' asked a lean-jawed detective.

'Only two that I ever knew about. One is a young lady, who lives in that apartment across the street, and the other –'

'Clare Nolan?' asked the officer quickly.

'Yes. The other is a Mr. Welden. I think he is a lawyer.'

The detective smiled knowingly and turned to a uniformed policeman.

'Go across the street and get the lady.'

'What's the name – Welden? Know him, Jimmy?'

The other plain-clothes man nodded. 'Harold Welden. Was with Hanley, Davidson and Hanley for quite a while. Got an office of his own now. Quite a mixer.'

'See if you can locate him, Jim.'

The plain-clothes man left the room and drove swiftly away, while the rest of the officers examined the room. While they were examining some of the old man's personal effects, Clare Nolan came in with the officer who had gone to her apartment.

She was tall, slender, wearing a black dress, which was severely plain, accenting the pallor of her white skin. Her hair was black, her features as clear-cut as a cameo. Just now her dark eyes were wide with apprehension as she saw the figure of the old man on the floor.

13

The policeman had merely told her that an old friend had met with an accident.

'Miss Nolan?' queried the detective, and she nodded, grasping for the back of a chair.

'What happened?' she asked in a whisper.

'Somebody bumped off the old man,' said a policeman gruffly.

'Killed him?' she gasped.

'Deader than a smoked herrin', lady. Better set down.'

Clare sank into a chair, staring at the huddled figure on the floor. The detective looked over her quizzically.

'You know him pretty well, Miss Nolan?'

'Yes, I – I knew him well.'

'That's what we want to know. When did you see him last?'

'Yesterday.'

'You didn't see him tonight?'

'No.'

'What do you know about him? Where is he from and what is his business?'

Clare shook her head 'He never told me anything about himself. I think he used to be in Arizona, because he used to tell me about that country.'

'Had plenty money, eh?'

'Money? No, I don't think he did. Oh, he had enough to live on. He was too old to work.'

14

'Not related to you in any way?'

'No, sir. He was a quaint old man, and I – I liked him. He seemed so lonely.'

The officer lighted a cigar and took several puffs.

'Never said anything to you about a will, did he?'

Clare shook her head quickly. 'No, he never spoke of one.'

'Do you know a lawyer by the name of Welden?'

Clare looked up quickly. 'Harold Welden? Yes, I know him.'

'Was he a friend of the old man?'

'They knew each other.'

'Welden ever do any legal work for him?'

'I'm sure I can't answer that question. Mr. Cleland never told me anything about himself.'

The arrival of the coroner stopped further questioning. The policeman beckoned to Clare, and she went with him to another room.

'Better for you than stayin' in there,' said the officer.

Clare thanked him and sat down.

'Do they want me for anything else?' she asked.

'I dunno, ma'am.'

The coroner was there at least fifteen

minutes, and as he was leaving, the detective arrived with Harold Welden, who had been drinking heavily. The detective had told Welden about the murder; so there was no need of any explanation. Welden didn't see Clare in the other room.

'Who shot him?' blurted Welden angrily.

'Rather a leading question this early in the game,' said the detective. 'This man was a friend of yours, Welden?'

'You might say he was. I knew him pretty well.'

'Ever do any legal work for him?'

Welden lifted his brows slightly and cleared his throat.

'No, I never have, officer.'

'Just a casual acquaintance, eh?'

'I've known him nearly two years.'

'When did you see him last?'

Welden deliberated with an owlish expression.

'Coupla days ago, I think,' he lied easily. No use telling the truth.

'Did you know he was wealthy?'

'Wealthy?' Welden laughed harshly. 'No, I didn't know he was. But what's the use of all this? Why not find the man who killed him?'

'Did you ever hear him say he was afraid of anyone?'

'No. I don't think he was. Tell me more

16

about how he was killed. I didn't get much of it.'

'Do you know Clare Nolan?'

Welden jerked slightly. 'Yes, I know her. What's she got to do with it?'

'Not a thing,' replied the detective, smiling a little, 'except that the old man lived long enough to scrawl out a will on a torn sheet of paper, in which he left everything he owned to this Clare Nolan. Here it is.'

Welden took the stained piece of paper and read the will, his jaw sagging a little.

'Lucky thing,' said the detective, 'that he upset the table when he fell, and knocked the ink and a pen to the floor within reach. He couldn't have lived long.'

The officer had spoken loud enough for Clare to hear, and when Welden looked up, Clare was standing in front of him, staring at the torn piece of paper in his hands. Welden didn't say anything as Clare took the paper from his hand and read it through. There were tears in her eyes as she realized that her old friend had used up his few remaining moments in penning that epistle. The tragedy of the splatter from the broken pen at the period of the postscript; the crimson smear across the bottom, where the heel of his old hand had rested. She looked up at the officer, a sharp catch in her voice.

'He – he knew who killed him. Oh, why didn't he tell us?'

The officer shook his head slowly. He had grown gray in the service, and he knew much about human nature.

'That man was one of the old-timers,' he said slowly. 'An old Arizona cowman. They look at things a bit different, I guess. They never went in very strong for the law. If an enemy shot them down, they – well, the breaks were against them. Punishment didn't mean much, unless they could administer it. This man knew who killed him, but he didn't squeal. As long as he couldn't pay back the score, he don't want the law to do it. Possibly this ends an old feud, and we'll never know who killed him.'

'That's right,' mumbled Welden. 'Somebody laid for him. Maybe it was somebody from Arizona. Do you want me for anything else, officer?'

'No, I guess not.'

Welden turned to Clare. 'I'll take you home,' he said.

Clare shook her head quickly.

'I am going to stay here until they take him away.'

'Oh, don't be foolish. You can't do anything for him.'

'I am not asking for any advice, Mr.

Welden. I'll stay, if the officers do not object.'

'I'll not object,' smiled the detective, 'and I think it's kind of you to want to stay. Good-evening, Mr. Welden.'

And Harold Welden walked out, without a backward glance.

'Drunk as a fool,' grunted a policeman.

'The ambulance ought to be here pretty quick, Chief.'

'Must have been out on a job.'

He turned to Clare. 'You've got that will, Miss Nolan?'

'Yes.'

'Keep it. Nobody can bust that kind of a will. Take it to a sober lawyer and have it filed for probate.'

'Do you really think it amounts to anything? I mean, do you suppose he was in his right mind? Hurt as he was, he might have imagined –'

'Lady, that will was written by a man with a clear mind. He died at the finish. He's got more than that Arizona ranch, because he merely includes that. Here comes the ambulance. Frank, escort the lady back where you found her.'

'Anything to work on?' asked the detective who had brought Welden.

'Not a thing, Jim. Looks like revenge.

Maybe it started years ago. Somebody from Arizona. Let's go.'

CHAPTER II

Frank Welden was not the type of man to inspire confidence. He was tall and thin, almost to the point of emaciation. His bony head was covered with a thin growth of black hair, his clean-shaven, lean jaws showed the blue of hidden beard through his skin, and on the back of his scrawny neck the hair sprouted at length. His nose was long and rather thin, pinched at the bridge from wearing glasses, through which peered keen eyes.

Welden was rather an old-timer in Cinco City. At the time of the mining boom he had conducted an assay office, also specialized in buying and selling stock, prospects and partly developed mines. It was said that Welden had made plenty of money, and it was also hinted that much of it had been made in crooked dealing with the prospectors.

At any rate, Welden made enough money to buy an interest in the Cinco City Bank, where he became cashier. Cool, calculating, cold-blooded, devoid of sentiment, as impersonal as one of his own inkstands, he stood between the patrons and the bank, always demanding the pound of flesh. Cinco City was no metropolis, and the bank was no thriving institution, but it paid well enough, because there was no outstanding stock. Welden owned half, and the other half was owned by Sig Heffron, retired cattleman, who lived in Sacramento and dabbled in politics.

Cinco City had never grown any beyond its boom days. It was the county seat and some of the trains stopped there on schedule. It was a cattle-shipping point for Cinco Valley, as well as an outfitting point. The main street was two blocks long, slightly crooked, always dusty. Few of the false-fronted buildings followed any definite line, except that some of them threatened at any time to topple forward into the street. The wooden sidewalks were narrow. Nail-heads protruded from them to trip the unwary, and in spots they swayed like a suspension bridge. The courthouse was a two-story building, a boxlike structure, minus any semblance of paint. Hitch-racks lined the streets, and the only shade was afforded by the wooden porches or wooden awnings, from which the pitch oozed and dripped during the summer. About two miles and a half north of the town was the JHC connected outfit, and adjoining that on the northeast side was the J Bar 44, the main ranch buildings being about a mile and half apart. About three miles east of Cinco City was the Tomahawk outfit, owned by Tom Hawker. Two miles southwest was the Circle Dot, known locally as the 'Doughnut' outfit, for the reason that the dot inside the circle was of such proportions as to cause the band greatly to resemble a doughnut. Eight miles below the Circle Dot, and on the same road, was the little town of Aztec Wells.

Cinco River ran southwest, its nearest point within a mile of Cinco City, where it swerved to the southeast nearly to the Circle Dot, where the wagon-road followed close to it all the way to Aztec Wells. If the river had ever run bankful, it would have floated a Leviathan, with feet to spare, but it never did. Only in the early spring did it go on a rampage, and later it degenerated into a lot of ill-smelling pools, where even the cattle did not care to drink.

Water was worth its weight in gold in the Cinco River range in the hot weather. Springs were jealously guarded. It was said that water had caused more killings in Cinco City than whiskey.

'Panamint' Pelley was the sheriff, a short, chubby person, with a pair of buffalo-horn mustaches, mild, inquiring eyes, and a touch

22

of rheumatism. His deputy was a tall, thin, sad-eyed person, with flaring ears, sandy hair, and a long nose, slightly out of line with the rest of his face. He had been christened William Dudley Day, but he was known by everyone as 'Melancholy.' The personal appearance of sheriff and deputy had long been a source of argument between them.

'I wouldn't be as fat as you are f'r anythin',' declared Melancholy. 'Man, you're jist round, thasall.'

'Well, I'm glad I'm not as flat as you are,' retorted Panamint. 'You ain't givin' yore insides no chance. I'll betcha yore lungs looks like a couple smoked herrin' hangin' up by the tail, and yore heart's shaped like a lead pencil. You look t' me like one of them Maniller envelopes that got stuck by mistake.'

While Panamint and Melancholy were arguing, 'Pima' Simpson and 'Elastic' Jones were on their way to town from the JHC.

It was hot on this certain day in Cinco City. Not that heat was any novelty, of course, but it seemed to bother Henry Elastic Jones more than usual. All his life had been spent in the Southwest, and Elastic Jones was past sixty, and to hear him sing his own praises, 'The best dern cook between the two Poles.'

That covered quite a lot of territory, as Pima Simpson had often stated. Old Pima was past sixty, admitted thirty-five, and was kept on at the JHC as a sort of horse-wrangler. A broken leg, which had been clumsily set, ruined Pima as a top-hand, but he wouldn't admit it.

They were a hard-bitten old couple, riding down a dusty road toward Cinco City; going to town with their wages, promising each other to stay as sober as a judge, and probably would end up as drunk as a pair of boiled owls – if boiled owls do get drunk.

'A man's as old as he feels – and I'm sixteen t'day,' declared Pima.

' 'F it wasn't f'r this damned heat allatime,' complained Elastic. 'Seems like I never do git used to it. I don't mind kitchen heat. That kinda heat jist skids off me; but this sun –'

Old Elastic shoved his floppy sombrero on the back of his head, and sang mournfully:

> 'Lotta barren hills,
> Awful danged sunny,
> Lotta dam' work,
> And not much money.

> 'Rather be a Eskimo,
> With a big, fat wife,
> Gittin' cooled off
> F'r once in m' life.'

'Heat makes yuh sentimental, Elastic,' drawled Pima. 'How come yuh never got married?'

'Married? Well, f'r gosh sakes! Ain't I?'

'I'm givin' yuh time to think out a good lie.'

'Lie? Pima, I've done been married three times in m' life.'

'Yuh don't need to stretch the truth allatime. Twice would have been enough.'

'Been enough f'r me, too. The first time was a Arapajo kid. Gave her pa six horses that I stole from the Sioux, and we was married Injun fashion. I kinda liked this here gal, and not havin' a hell of a lot of faith in Injun marriages, I tuck her to a justice of the peace and got married ag'in. Then she got monkeyin' around a church, where there was some converted Injuns, and the first thing I knowed she was askin' for a priest weddin'. Cost me five dollars. Then I lost her.'

'Died on yuh, Elastic?'

'No-o-o-o. Got civilized and ran away with a sheepherder.'

'Uh-huh. Soured you ag'in wimmin, I reckon.'

'Soured me ag'in sheepherders, too.'

'Here comes some of that dam' Gavin outfit, th'owin' plenty dust.'

The two old men, riding slowly, reined off to the side of the road, as four men rode

25

swiftly past, showering them with a cloud of dust. The four men ignored the two, as they raced on toward Cinco City.

'Some day,' declared Elastic, spitting out dust, 'I'm goin' to hang Chuck Gavin on the hot end of a bullet.'

'Not to mention old Bat Gavin and their lovely relative, Dicky Ellers,' said Pima, red-eyed from the dust. 'That was Chuck, Dick, Dan McKenna, and Scotty Gleason. Act like they owned the whole dam' road. Why didja pull out to the side?'

'Follerin' you. Whatsa matter with yuh, Pima? Are you scared of 'em.'

'I ain't scared of no danged man. Some sweet day I'll –'

'Pull out ag'in. I wish Old Million Dollar would come back here. All I want is a chance at them Gavins, but they won't start nothin', except with the old man – and him settin' down there in Los Angylees, takin' life easy. Guns up Old Jim Gavin, easy as yuh please, and then walks out to keep from killin'. Says he don't want no feuds; don't want none of his men t' mix up in the trouble. I betcha them danged J Bar 44's are stealin' our cows.'

'Betcha they are,' nodded Pima. 'I done spoke to Ted Bell about it, and he snapped m' head off. Asked me if I was tryin' to start trouble.'

26

'Ted's all right. I talked with Larry Delago about it, and he said he thought we was losin' cattle, but there wasn't no evidence who was gittin' 'em. I wouldn't trust Gavin as far as I could th'ow a bull by the tail. They hate our outfit, and I wonder how comes that some of 'em ain't gone down to Los Angylees and gunned up the old man. Bat Gavin swore he'd kill Million Dollar f'r shootin' Jim. Old Bat ain't so danged fast with a gun; not like Chuck is, of course. Mebby Chuck ain't feudin' ag'in Million Dollar, bein' as Old Jim was only his uncle, but I wouldn't bank on it. There's still that spring to keep 'em sore, yuh know.'

'I don't hold with no feuds,' said Pima. 'Let sleepin' dogs lie. But if any man steps up and chooses me – I'm Johnny at the rat-hole.'

'Me – I'll shoot it out with any of 'em.'

'Yeah, I know. Yo're dangerous – in more ways'n one. I know that danged well, every time I look at the grub you cook for us.'

'Yea-a-a-ah! Well, 'f I was as old as you are, and m' teeth was played out, I'd kick on men-food m'self, I suppose.'

They tied their horses at a hitch-rack away from that occupied by the four J Bar 44 horses, and went into the Cinco City bar, which was the largest place of its kind in the country. Several games were running, and the bartender was busy with thirsty customers.

27

The four men from Gavin's ranch were at the bar, laughing and drinking.

But Chuck Gavin wasn't one of them. A tow-headed, stub-nosed cowboy, 'Bud' McCoy, was the fourth member. Pima had mistaken him for Chuck Gavin, as they were about the same build. Dick Ellers, Chuck Gavin's cousin, was a swaggering sort of cowboy, well built, swarthy, sporting a small mustache. Ellers was rather good-looking, except that his eyes were too small and narrow for the size of his face, giving him a sleepy appearance.

The Cinco range was well represented in there. Tony Dunham, 'Pecan' Cassidy, and Andy Tolliver were there from the Circle Dot, Tom Hawker and Mike Joe, a half-breed Navajo and Apache, from the Tomahawk, and several cowboys from ranches down around Aztec. Tom Hawker was a tall, rangy, hawk-faced man, with deep-set eyes beneath bristling brows. His cheek-bones were extremely prominent, and his jaw jutted belligerently. But he was a man who minded his own business. He had owned the Tomahawk three years. It was rumored that Hawker was of part aboriginal blood, because his brother, Pete Hawker, looked like an Indian, and because their two men, 'Lobo' Wolf and Mike Joe, were both half-breeds.

28

The two old boys from the JHC leaned against the bar and began taking on their cargo of liquor. Everyone was in good humor and much liquor flowed. Melancholy Day came in and looked over the crowd with a critical eye. Payday might bring trouble – it usually did – and Melancholy didn't want to see any of the boys get hurt.

'Hello, old killjoy,' greeted Pima. 'C'mon and have a drink, Melancholy.'

Melancholy shook his head sadly. 'Gotta keep sober t'day, Pima.'

'Have somethin' soft, then.'

'Well, thasall right – gimmie some gin.'

Melancholy drank his gin straight and without a grimace.

'I hate them soft drinks,' he said sadly, 'but I've gotta keep sober on payday. How's everythin' at the ranch?'

'Purty good,' admitted Pima.

'Hear anythin' from Million Dollar lately?'

'Not for about a year. He's still down there in the city.'

'Los Angylees,' said Elastic Jones, who seemed to like the name. 'Wisht he'd come home. I tell yuh, Melancholy' – Elastic cleared his throat and lowered his voice – 'we're losin' cows. Somebody is liftin' critters on us.'

'Pshaw!' grunted the deputy, unimpressed. 'Ain't no reasonable chance for that to come

29

about. Yuh can't graft wings on 'em, and that's the only way yuh could git away with 'em.'

Elastic nodded and ordered more drinks. Melancholy took gin.

'There's a shrinkage,' said Pima. 'I don't account f'r it. Ain't none of my business, but jist the same I wrote a letter t' Million Dollar and I said I had plenty suspicions. Million Dollar writes me a letter, in which he says the weather is fine down there, but he writes Ted Bell a letter and says f'r him not to start any trouble with Gavin. Ted Bell didn't. Ted's a hell of a good cowman, but I think he's lackin' in entrails. 'F I was foreman, I'd shore make that J Bar 44 awful hard to catch.'

'Ted's right,' said Melancholy. 'Let's have another drink. Gimmie more of that watery-lookin' stuff. I like it better'n sody, I think. Kinda bites.'

The bartender treated, and then the men each bought another round, whereupon the bartender treated again.

'Pretty hot t'day,' complained Elastic. 'Dang such a country.'

Melancholy cuffed his hat sideways on his lean head and stared at Elastic.

'Don' shay that,' he said owlishly. 'Bes' li'l country on earth.'

'Whassamatter 'ith you?' queried Pima.

30

'You ain't drunk!'

Melancholy turned his back to the bar, cuffed his hat to the other side of his head, and goggled at the opposite wall.

'I sh'd shay not! Drunk? Haw, haw, haw, haw! On what, I'd crave to know.'

He turned around, facing the bar, giggling to himself.

'Le's shing a shong.'

'Yuh hadn't ort to sing,' advised the bartender. 'If Panamint sees yuh, he might get sore.'

'Tha's per'ly all right, now. What'll we shing?'

'Lemme see,' said Pima. He cocked one eye on the ceiling, making a desperate effort to remember a song. 'I've got her,' he announced. He opened his mouth, took a deep breath and began mournfully, 'O-o-o-o-o-oh, why do you wait, de-e-e-ear bro-o-o-o-o-ther-r-r-r –'

'You're from the JHC, ain't you?' Pima closed his mouth and looked reprovingly at a man who had come in beside him. It was the depot agent.

'Here's a telegram,' he said, and handed it to Pima.

The man grinned and walked out, with Pima staring after him. Pima's jaw sagged a little, and Melancholy fought his hat for a moment.

'A telegram,' said Pima in an awed voice. 'My gosh, that's bad news. You take it, Elastic,' holding it out to him.

'Nossir,' Elastic shook his head violently. 'It ain't t' me.'

'Well,' Pima swallowed heavily. 'I dunno. Who's it from? That's what gits me. Why didn't that dam' fool tell us somethin'? Jist hands it t' me and says, "Here's a telegram." What do I know about telegrams? I tell yuh, that ain't no way to do. You take it, Melancholy.'

'Not me, pardner. Why don'tcha open it and see who it's from?'

'Well – yea-a-a-ah.'

Pima's hands trembled as he drew forth the yellow sheet, which he crumpled in his hand as he turned to the bartender.

'Give us a little drink,' he said hoarsely. 'This calls f'r one.'

They drank solemnly, after which Pima laid the paper on the bar, and they all read it.

'Why, she's f'r Ted Bell!' exploded Pima. 'Thank gosh, she ain't f'r me! Read her out loud, Melancholy.'

Melancholy proceeded to do so.

TED BELL, CINCO CITY, ARIZONA.
UNDERSTAND JOHN H. CLELAND SHOT
AND KILLED LAST NIGHT BY UNKNOWN
ASSAILANT STOP WROTE WILL BEFORE
DYING LEAVING ALL HIS PROPERTY TO
GIRL CLARE NOLAN WHO WILL BRING
BODY TO CINCO CITY FOR BURIAL AND TO
PROBATE WILL THERE STOP BODY MUST BE
IDENTIFIED THERE STOP WILL ADVISE DATE
OF ARRIVAL STOP NOTIFY FRANK WELDEN.

HAL WELDEN

'John H. Cleland?' whispered Pima. 'Old
Million Dollar?'

'That's what she says,' whispered
Melancholy. 'Poor Ol' Million Dollar.'

'Dead?' grunted Elastic. 'Ol' Million
Dollar? My gosh!'

Elastic's voice boomed in the saloon, and
the men began crowding around, questioning
the three men. Tom Hawker read the telegram
aloud to the men.

They had all known Old Million Dollar
Cleland.

'That's shore tough,' said Dick Ellers.

'Prob'ly saves you and the Gavins,' retorted
old Pima hotly.

Ellers flushed, but did not reply. Pima was
broken-hearted and mad. There had been
a close bond between Pima and Cleland,

33

shared by Elastic Jones. Elastic was just drunk enough to cry unashamed.

'Stop it!' ordered Melancholy. 'I hate cryin' folks. Oh, gawsh, you make me tired, Elastic! 'F a man's dead, he's dead, ain't he? Whatsa use of yuh runnin' all yo're tears on the bar? They say a man's ninety per cent water, and yo're not over thirty per cent man right now. Quit it, before we have to pick yuh up on a mop, you danged fool!'

Ted Bell, foreman of the JHC, came striding in, followed by Larry Delago and Mose Heilman, JHC punchers. Bell was a good-looking cowboy, a little over average size, lithe and wiry, about thirty years of age. The lines of his face were a little deep for a man of his age, and he had a passion for poker.

Delago was about as tall as Bell, thin, dark of skin, lean-faced. His nose was long and thin, but his nostrils flared widely, and his brown eyes were habitually flecked with red. He wore his hair long in front of his ears, and he wore a scarlet muffler around his throat, a clash of color against his grass-green silk shirt.

Heilman was a flat-faced blond, with a generous nose and small, blue eyes; a colorless sort of a person. All three men wore leather chaps, belts, and holstered guns.

34

Bell knew something had gone wrong, when he entered the saloon. One of the men handed him the telegram and he scowled heavily, his jaw tightening, as he looked at them.

'This seems to be for me,' he said shortly.

'Pima opened it by mistake,' said the bartender quickly.

'Yea-a-ah?' Bell looked at Pima.

'What is it, Ted?' asked Delago.

'The old man's been killed,' said Ted evenly.

'Old man Cleland?' asked Heilman quickly, and Ted nodded.

'That's the worst news I ever heard,' said Pima.

Bell's eyes swept the room.

'You've all read it?' he asked.

'Hawker read it out loud,' said someone.

Bell nodded slowly, turned to Pima, as though to say something, but stopped and turned to the bar.

'I'll buy a drink for everybody,' he said.

The crowd moved over to the bar, where they filled their glasses.

Ted Bell lifted his glass, possibly intending to offer a toast, but Old Pima boomed, 'Boys, here's to the best friend I ever had, the best man that ever died with his boots on – Million Dollar Cleland.'

'A square shooter,' added Elastic.

'And a straight shooter,' said Dick Ellers seriously.

'Wherever he is,' said Ted Bell, and they drank their liquor with a slight flourish.

The four men from the J Bar 44 walked out of the place. Bell paid for the drinks, put the telegram in his pocket, and went over to the bank. Old Pima backed against the bar, ruminating to himself, and the games went on. They had paid their respects to an old-timer.

'And a straight shooter,' muttered Pima. 'Dick Ellers said that.'

'He shore was,' sighed Elastic, sobered by the news. 'What did it say about Old Million Dollar leavin' everythin' to a woman? Yuh don't s'pose he fell fer a woman – at his age?'

'Looks thataway,' sighed Elastic. 'No fool like an old one. Me an' you'll soon be takin' our how-dee-doo-o-o-o from a petticoat. Please t' meetcha, Mister Jones. Pick me a flower, will yuh? I can't stand f'r a man that drinks.'

'Mister Jones, will yuh please wash yore face and hands, before yuh put that chuck on the table? Life' – Pima paused thoughtfully – 'is jist goin' to be too sweet f'r me and you, Elastic.'

'I ain't stayin'. Ain't never cooked f'r no dam' woman – and I won't.'

36

'She'll prob'ly want us t' tie blue ribbons on the tails of our cows, instead of brandin' 'em.'

Pecan Cassidy, a small snub-nosed, freckled cowboy, came over to them.

'Sure hard luck,' he said sympathetically. 'Uncle Bill will sure be sorry to hear about it.'

Pima nodded sadly. Uncle Bill Haskell, owner of the Circle Dot, was an old friend of John Cleland.

'Struck me kinda funny – them Gavin punchers, drinkin' a toast to him,' said Cassidy.

'Yeah, it was,' admitted Pima. 'Still and all, Dick Ellers was only a nephew to Jim Gavin. Might have been different if Chuck or his dad had been here.'

'Chuck's over on the Coast,' said Cassidy. 'Been away a week or more.'

'Yea-a-ah? Whereabouts on the Coast?'

'Frisco or Los Angeles, I think.'

'Yea-a-ah? Huh!'

Pima thought this over quite a while. He and Elastic had lost all desire for liquor. Melancholy had wandered away, loaded with gin.

'Let's go back to the ranch,' said Elastic. 'I'm kinda soured on hooch.'

'So'm I. C'mon.'

They went out to the hitch-rack, where

37

they mounted and rode back toward the JHC; two old men, riding knee to knee along a dusty road, hats drawn low over their eyes.

'Unknown a-sailin' t' hell!' snorted Pima angrily.

'What didja say?' asked Elastic.

'Nothin' – I was jist thinkin' out loud.'

CHAPTER III

'How would it be if I called the porter and had him bring us each a nice cold drink, eh?'

Clare Nolan had been watching the uninteresting landscape from the dusty car window, absorbed in her own thoughts, but now she looked up quickly. A big man, florid, with red-rimmed eyes almost concealed in puffs of fat, was leaning across the end of the seat, smirking at her. He was odorous with perfume and bad liquor.

Twice before that day he had tried to approach her, but she had ignored him; now he was back again, smelling stronger of liquor than ever. There were only three other occupants of the sleeper, an oldish couple

38

farther up the car, both of them apparently asleep, and a youngish man across the aisle, who seemed absorbed in a magazine. The young man was well built, with a shapely head of crisp, curly brown hair, level blue eyes. His skin was tanned. He was not handsome, but there was a devil-may-care expression on his strong features.

As the big man spoke to Clare, the young man turned his head slightly and looked at them, apparently uninterested in either of them. Clare turned her head, ignoring the invitation to drink, and the big man glanced across the aisle with a smirking wink. He turned back to Clare.

'Don't be a prude,' he said rather loud. 'We're all good little friends together. Thaw out, sister. Let's have a drink and then I'll buy you breakfast.'

'I am perfectly able to buy my own meals,' she said coldly. 'Please go away and do not annoy me.'

The man laughed softly and sat down on the arm of the seat.

'I'm a perfectly reliable citizen,' he said. 'Name's Grover Harris, and I sell jewelry for Bryan and Sneed of Chicago. Everybody along the line knows little Grover. Sells more jewels than any two men. Had a big sale on this trip, and I'm willing to buy you something. Be a good fellow.'

But Clare ignored him. He looked at the young man, winked owlishly, and shrugged his shoulders. The young man looked him over thoughtfully. Grover Harris sighed deeply and spoke across the aisle.

'Why don't *you* try your luck with her,' he said sneeringly.

The young man smiled softly, as he marked his place in the magazine. Without any undue haste he arose from his seat, and jerked his head toward the rear of the car. The big man grinned, got ponderously to his feet, and led the way. They disappeared behind the curtained entrance to the washroom,and Clare drew a sigh of relief.

It was growing darker now. The conductor had told her that they would arrive late at Cinco City – possibly about ten o'clock. In the baggage-car of that train was the body of John H. Cleland, going back to rest in the little cemetery on the hill. Hal Welden had told her that they would be on hand to take charge of the funeral arrangements. She had given up her position. Investigation of Cleland's effects showed that he had over fifty thousand dollars invested in stocks and bonds, presumably in care of the Cinco City Bank. Of actual cash there was less than five hundred. Of course, Clare would get none of

40

this until the will had been probated.

Hal Welden had not pressed his suit any further. Possibly he knew it was no use, because Clare had told him she did not admire a drunkard nor a gambler – and he was both. She did not ask him to handle any of her affairs. They met at the inquest, which was a perfunctory affair, both testifying to what they knew about the old man, and the usual verdict was rendered.

Clare had always lived in a city, knew nothing about the ways of the range country except what she had read and what Cleland had told her, and now she wondered what it would be like.

The young man sauntered back from the washroom and she looked up at him, but he seemed absorbed in his own affairs, and sat down with his magazine. In a few moments the porter hurried up the aisle, stopped by the young man and said something in a low, agitated tone. The young man merely smiled and went on reading, while the porter gave Clare a searching glance, and went back to the washroom. She wondered what had gone wrong. Presently the big man lumbered out into the aisle, bracing himself against the surge of the train, and came up the aisle.

He was what might be termed 'a mess.' His face was streaked with blood and water, his

41

nose was swollen twice its normal size, and one eye was almost swollen shut. He carried his collar and tie, wet and bedraggled, in his hand, and his hair looked as though someone had held his head under a faucet.

He looked straight ahead as he passed Clare and the young man, heading for his own seat midway of the car, where he flopped down. The young man lowered his magazine and studied the actions of the big man. Clare had seen the condition of the big man, and she wondered what could have happened to him.

Just now he was evidently opening a bag, judging from his actions. Suddenly the young man got to his feet, and in a few catlike steps was in behind the big man, looking over his shoulder. One glance, a swift grab with his left hand, and the young man stepped back, holding a silver-plated revolver in his hand. The big man started to protest, but sank back.

Dropping the gun in a side pocket of his coat, the young man came back to his seat, where he picked up his magazine. The big man slumped down, holding a handkerchief to his swollen features. Mile after mile clicked along. The young man rolled a cigarette and walked back to the washroom, but the big man stayed in his seat. The porter came

42

along, stopping near Clare, and she turned to him.

'What happened to the big man, porter?' she asked softly.

The Negro scratched his kinky head for a moment, a queer smile on his lips.

'Ma'am' Ah je's don't know. Ah didn't see de beginnin', but Ah seen de finish. Dis yere young man mus' have socked him powerful ha'd, 'cause he's sho' goggle-eyed, and den Ah hears dis young man sayin', "Next time you'll sho' know enough to let a lady alone," and den he kersocks him plenty ha'd. Yes, ma'am – plenty ha'd.'

Clare leaned back in her seat, puzzled and confused. She had thought these two men were friends, judging from the way they had gone back there together, but now she knew that the young man had merely taken him back there quietly to administer punishment. And the big man had intended using that revolver. Clare shuddered. She was grateful, of course, but rather amazed at the cool way in which the young man had performed. She wondered if she should thank him.

The engine was sounding a station whistle, and they soon drew in at a little town, where a blinking light on the depot showed the word TEJUNGA. She looked at her time-table. The next stop would be Cinco City. Just

43

beyond the depot on a sidetrack was a long string of cattle cars. It was a blind siding, where a cattle train had pulled in to allow the pasenger to pass.

The train made a short stop at Tejunga. It was a decidedly upgrade from Tejunga to Cinco City, and they traveled slowly. The young man came from the washroom and placed his valise on the seat. He looked at his watch, sat down, and stared out through the window. Clare wondered if he was getting off at Cinco City.

They were about two miles from Tejunga, when the whistle shrieked, and the train slowed down quickly. It came to a jolting stop. Clare peered out, but was unable to see anything wrong. They were stopped for possibly two or three minutes, when the engine began puffing again. Clare peered out again, and she could see enough to show that they were traveling backward. They could not hear the engine now, but the *clickety-clicks* of the rail joints were coming closer together as the train gathered speed. The coach began to rock badly. Suddenly the young man sprang to his feet, grasping the back of his seat.

'Train's busted in two,' he said calmly, 'and there's a cattle train following us.'

A brakeman came running down the aisle, his lantern bumping the seats as he ran.

'Broke in two?' asked the man.

'Think so. Holdup or something. Did you hear the shots?'

'No.'

'If that freight is still in the hole, and they see a light, they might throw that switch. God help the whole bunch, if they don't.'

He went running down the car, and they heard the doors banging behind him.

Clare was unable to speak. The young man looked at her, a smile on his lips.

'No use bein' scared, ma'am,' he said. 'There's two cars between us and the rear end, and that freight won't be comin' fast. Might as well set down and take it easy.'

'We are going faster all the time,' she whispered.

'Shore. Stiff grade. Straight track, though. If we can get past Tejunga, we hit an upgrade for a long ways – but I'm afraid they'll cut us off. Well, no use crossin' a bridge until yuh come to it.'

Grover Harris was out in the aisle, hanging on with both hands, looking toward them.

'What'll we do?' he bellowed. 'This is awful! What can I do?'

'Yuh might try jumpin' off,' said the young man calmly. 'If yuh don't like to jump – try prayin'. I reckon one would do yuh as much good as the other.'

45

'The railroad is responsible for us!'

'Fine! If we get killed, they're to blame. Set down and save yore legs.'

The door banged open, and passengers began crowding in. The brakeman had presence of mind enough to head the few passengers away from the rear of the train for greater safety in case of a bad smash. They were frightened badly, all trying to talk at once, clawing their way along, bumping each other.

When the crew of the cattle train backed into the blind siding at Tejunga to allow the passenger to pass, they discovered a hot-box on the car nearest the engine, and this discovery would delay them for some time. The brakeman cursed the antiquated piece of rolling stock, while the cowboys, accompanying the shipment of cattle, came up from the caboose to squat on their heels in the dark and watch them cool off the box.

The cattle were in charge of Buck Hogan, foreman of the Sawbuck outfit down at Sweetwater. Buck was short-handed and short-tempered as well. He was also short of stature, but long on conversation. They had left Sweetwater that morning, and it seemed to Buck that they had been sidetracked a dozen times.

'If we keep this up, we'll be in Chicago a year from this next fall,' he declared.

'Lucky we didn't cook that dam' wheel plumb off,' growled the brakeman. 'If we hadn't stopped when we did, you'd have lost some cows.'

Buck grunted and rolled a cigarette.

'Got time to go over and get a drink?' he asked. The brakeman grinned.

'Plenty. Number Six ain't through yet, and we'll be here an hour. Go ahead.'

The two cowboys with Buck followed him past the depot and down the narrow street of Tejunga to the first saloon. There were two men at the bar, but Buck paid no attention to them until he had poured himself a drink. He started to lift it to his lips, when he glanced into the fly-specked back-bar mirror, which reflected the image of a man at the bar. Slowly he lowered the drink and looked at the man.

He was tall, was this man at the bar, tall and thin, with a long, thin face, lazy gray eyes, and deeply carved features. Atop his head was a big tan-colored sombrero, and around his lean neck was a vermilion handkerchief. His blue shirt was faded from many washings, his vest little more than a string, and his bat-wing chaps showed signs of many trips through the chaparral and mesquite.

47

'Sad Sontag, or I'm a cow's uncle!' snorted Buck.

The tall man looked Buck over lazily. 'How are yuh, pardner? Long time I no see yuh.'

They shook hands solemnly, looking each over from boot to sombrero. Sontag's companion was shorter, broader of shoulder, blue-eyed, and with a decided Celtic cast of features. His sombrero was tilted over one eye, as he surveyed Buck gravely.

'Swede Harrigan, yuh ain't changed a bit,' said Buck slowly.

'What didja expect to see – an old man with a cane?' asked Swede.

'I dunno. Not seein' yuh f'r so danged long. Boys' – he turned to his two cowboys – 'these are Sad Sontag and Swede Harrigan from over in the Sundown country. You've heard me speak of 'em.'

'Plenty,' grinned Jimmy Miller. 'When Buck runs out of personal experiences, he starts lyin' about you two fellers.'

'I shore do,' stoutly. 'And not all of it are lies. But what are you two jiggers doin' over here so far from old Sundown?'

'We ain't been over there for more'n a year,' said Sontag. 'I sold out the TJ outfit quite a while ago, and then I served one term as sheriff, while Swede demonstrated to everybody that he wasn't a success at

48

raisin' horses on the Quarter Circle T; so we left Sundown and started driftin'. Been punchin' cows for an outfit up in the Piñon range country, but we didn't care much for 'em; so we drifted down here, thinkin' mebby we'd head down into the Sweetwater.'

'Why don'tcha do jist that?' asked Buck quickly. 'That's where my outfit is, and yuh sure got a pair of jobs right now. I've got a trainload of cows over on the tracks, headin' for Chicago. Got a hot axle; so we hived up here to let a passenger train through.'

'Well, that's fine,' grinned Sad. 'Mebby we will drift down there and hook up with yuh for a while. Anythin' excitin' going on down there?'

'Excitin'?' grinned Buck. 'Pardner, I kinda figures that the day of excitement in the cow country is at an end. We're gittin' civilized. There ain't no crooked work bein' done. All the cattle rustlers have gone to the legislature, and the gunmen have joined the army. Nossir, I tell yuh this here Western country is plumb docile. I often says to the boys – yuh see, I didn't know yuh was a sheriff over there – I says, "I wonder what Sad Sontag is doin' these days." I kinda pictured yuh over there, pickin' up potatoes. Not that Sundown was much of a place to raise potatoes, but you know what I mean.'

'It ain't what she used t' be,' admitted Sad. 'I wish we'd have a Injun uprisin' or somethin' like that. Crime is at a premium, as they say.'

'There jist ain't none,' declared Swede. 'Punchin' cows is just a job. Even the horses don't buck like they used to do. Don't seem to put their hearts into the job.'

'Ain't it true,' agreed Jimmy Miller. 'I can notice it.'

'Yea-a-a-ah!' snorted Buck. 'And neither does the puncher. Couple more seasons and we'll be sendin' to a mail-order house for our riders.'

Buck bought another drink, and they all went over to the train. The hot-box was cooled off, and as they sat there in the lantern light, Number Six came in, made a short stop, and went on toward Cinco City.

Buck and Sad talked of the days when they had been together, and Buck told him how he had acquired foremanship of the Sawbuck cattle outfit.

'Golly, I'm sure glad I ran into yuh here, Sad,' he said. 'I've been kinda short-handed for months, and you two fellers fit in fine. I'll send a telegram to the ranch, tellin' 'em t' look out for you fellers. You can step right in, jist as though I'm there. Right now we've got a lot of horses to break, and I don't know

50

of no better men to do the job. But yuh won't find no trouble to take yore mind off horses.'

'I'm not lookin' for trouble,' laughed Sad.

'You shore used to look for it.'

'Well, mebby I'm growin' up with the country, Buck.'

'Uh-huh. What ever became of that big sorrel yuh used to ride?'

'A rustler hung him on the hot end of a bullet coupla years ago.'

'Sure some bronc. Well, the boys will take good care of yuh both. I'll make that telegram good and strong. Mebby I better go over to the depot and send it right now. How much time have we got?' he asked the brakeman.

The brakeman grunted, 'Go ahead and take yore time,' he said; 'we won't pull out for fifteen minutes, anyway; and mebby by that time we'll be ordered to stay here for another half-hour, I dunno.'

Buck got up and started toward the depot, but stopped, looking up the track.

'What's this comin'?' he yelled.

The tracks were humming, and the men could hear the roar of a train. The two brakemen and the conductor sprang to their feet, and ran out to where they could look up the track. There was no train due from that direction. In fact, there had not been time for

51

Number Six to reach Cinco City and allow another train to pass.

But there was no doubt that a train was coming from toward Cinco City – and coming fast. The rear lights were visible now.

'My gosh, it's a runaway!' yelled the conductor. 'And that switch is open! They'll telescope our train, boys! Get away!'

The engine crew had seen it, and made their jump from the opposite side of the engine. The cowboys were running away from the train, along with the brakemen and conductor, scattering like a lot of quail. It was about three hundred feet from the switch to the end of the depot. There had been no time to throw that switch and keep the train on the main line; no time to do anything, except run out of the danger zone.

With a roar and a screech the rear car hit the switch, but it was going too fast to make the turn. There came a streak of flame, the scream of metal on metal, a cloud of dust, and the rear car shot across the points, probably tearing the switch to pieces, and five cars of that passenger train came careering across the carth straight toward the dcpot.

It was all over in a few watch-ticks. The air was full of dust, out of which gradually evolved the shapes of passenger coaches, still upright on their trucks, standing at all kinds

52

of queer angles, buried to their axles in the dirt. The platform of the rear car had crumpled against the rear of the depot platform, but not a car had overturned nor had any of them hit the cattle train.

Sad had nearly been caught by one of the hurtling cars, and the dust was still enveloping the wreck as he climbed over the smashed platform of the rear coach and went inside. It seemed that every window had been smashed, and the aisle was a jumble of seat cushions. But there was no one in the car; so he forced his way through the upper door, where he found the next car almost at right angles with Swede trying to force his way through a blocked door. But they found that car empty of human beings.

By that time the crew of the cattle train, augmented by the people of Tejunga, who had heard the crash, were forcing their way into other cars; so Sad and Swede climbed in with them. They found the passengers in one car. One or two women had fainted and a couple were screaming at the top of their voices. But there did not seem to be any seriously injured. They carried some of the women out, but most of them were able to walk.

Sad found Clare on the floor, a heavy cushion across her lap. She smiled up at him, as a brakeman held a lantern near them, and Sad helped her get up

'Hurt any?' he asked.

'I – I don't think so – just frightened. My, what a crash! And we – we knew it was coming – that was the worst of it all. I surely thought my last day had arrived. Was anybody killed?'

'Don't reckon there was, ma'am. Looks t' me like what you'd call a lucky wreck.'

A man pawed his way up from under a pile of cushions. It was Grover Harris, one eye swollen shut. He blinked at them with the other.

'I am Grover Harris,' he said dumbly. 'Best jewelry salesman on the road.'

'Yo're jist off the road now, pardner,' smiled Sad.

Harris stared blankly at Sad, picked up his smashed valise, and went staggering down the aisle.

'May as well get off, I suppose,' said the conductor, who had a bruised cheek and a wrenched arm. 'Thank gosh, it is no worse than this. I don't understand what happened.'

'Train broke in two?' asked Sad.

'Apparently.'

They climbed down and went over to the little depot. There was no doctor in the town, but luckily there were no serious injuries. The people of Tejunga were doing all they could to make everyone comfortable. The young man who had whipped the jewelry salesman was suffering from a knock on the head, but was able to walk around. He saw Clare with Sad Sontag, and came over to her.

'I've been lookin' for you,' he said. 'Didn't get hurt? Gee that's fine! The roof fell in on me, but I'm all right now.'

'Oh, I'm so glad you were not badly injured,' said Clare.

'Oh, we're a tough family,' he smiled and walked away.

'Shore is a tough family,' said a cowboy. 'They're all tough – them Gavins.'

'Do you know the Gavins?' asked Clare of Sad.

He shook his head quickly. 'I'm a stranger here,' he told her.

They went into the little waiting-room, where passengers were detailing their experiences, each one trying to talk louder than the rest. The telegraph operator was fairly burning up the wires, telling the division superintendent what had happened. Someone came in, yelling that the engine was coming down the track; so everyone tried to get out on the platform again.

The engine and baggage-car had stopped just short of the smashed switch, and the engine crew came running down the platform. The engineer was white beneath his coating of grime, as he stumbled into the light of the waiting-room. He stared at the conductor, who put a hand on his arm.

'Nobody killed, Roberts,' said the conductor. 'Nobody badly hurt. What went wrong?'

The engineer brushed a grimy hand across his forehead, as though trying to believe that everyone in that train had escaped death or severe injuries.

'Nobody badly hurt? It's a miracle! We were held up. Track blocked and a red signal out. There were two men, masked, and they had us covered almost before we stopped. Then they cut off the baggage-car – cut the air. I tried to tell them that the rest of the train would slip down the grade, but they wouldn't listen. Then they blew the safe, after shooting the messenger. He isn't dead, but he's badly hurt. I knew the switch was open, and with that stock train –'

'We split the switch,' said the conductor simply.

'Wrecker on the way, with doctors and nurses,' informed the operator. 'Give me the facts on this holdup; and I'll try to get action from Cinco City.'

The engineer went into the little office,

while the rest of them went over to the baggage-car and brought out the wounded messenger, who was unconscious. The through safe had been dynamited, and was on its back in the middle of the car.

'Won't be able to move our train for hours,' complained Buck. 'That track is all torn to hell out there. Prob'ly have to feed and water here, 'cause we won't get out until the track is fixed. Jist my darned luck. But you fellers go on down to the Sawbuck. I ain't sent that telegram yet, but there's plenty time.'

Sad tilted his sombrero down over his eyes, as he scratched the back of his head thoughtfully.

'Mebby yuh better not send it, Buck.'

'Yuh ain't goin' down there, Sad?'

'Not just yet. I've been thinkin' it over. Yuh see, there was a woman and kids on that train, and them dirty skunks knowed it. Wasn't no sense cuttin' that train loose thataway – sendin' folks to what shore looked like a certain death. Shootin' a messenger and robbin' a train is bad enough – but yuh can overlook things like that. Sendin' folks hellin' down a grade – well, I'd kinda like to stop around here awhile and see if I can't help a little to keep them same men from doin' anythin' like that again.'

57

'I know how yuh feel. When I was climbin' into them cars, expectin' to find a lot of folks dead and dyin' – I git sweaty yet.'

'Uh-huh. And if you'll keep them jobs open –'

'They're always open. I wish I could stay and help yuh, but them cows shore need a chambermaid, and – anyway, I saved the price of a telegram.'

'Thank yuh, Buck – and so-long.'

'Good luck.'

And they faded out in the darkness, heading for the livery stable.

CHAPTER IV

Melancholy Day, deputy sheriff of Cinco City, was mad. He sat on the edge of his cot in the rear of the sheriff's office and swore sinfully. The air was redolent of something very obnoxious, and Melancholy knew what it was. His long nose twitched violently and his sad eyes glared balefully.

Not only that, but Melancholy was ten dollars loser. He had met with skulduggery, but he couldn't prove it. Ward Bellew and Andy Tolliver, of the Doughnut outfit, were the culprits. Bellew was short and fat, with an innocent mien. Tolliver was lanky, sorrel-topped, with a crooked nose and a big mouth.

It began with an argument between Bellew and Melancholy; an argument started by Bellew, who knew that Melancholy would bet on anything. Mind-reading was the subject of the argument, and Melancholy had scoffed at the idea of a man being able to read another man's mind. Bellew swore that Tolliver, as ignorant as he was, could do it.

'Betcha ten dollars he can't do no such a dam' thing,' said Melancholy.

Bellew protested. He didn't want Melancholy's money. It was the old 'common' game, but Melancholy didn't know it. The argument grew hotter, until Tolliver was appealed to to prove Bellew's statement.

'Aw, I can do it,' said Tolliver, 'but I ain't so awful good.'

'Yuh can, eh?' grunted Melancholy. 'Betcha ten dollars yuh can't.'

'Put up yore money,' yawned Bellew. 'Here's mine. Let the bartender hold stakes. Now, we've got to make this test so that everybody can know. Andy is right. I'll tell yuh what we'll do. Andy will go outside, where he can't hear what's said. You pick out some numbers, and we'll write 'em on a piece of paper. Then Andy will come in and tell yuh what the numbers are.'

'All right. Send one of the boys with him; so there won't be no chance for him to hear.'

Larry Delago, of the JHC outfit, went out with Andy, while Melancholy decided on the figures. All the conversation was carried on in low tones, the numbers written on a piece of paper, and then Andy was called in.

He leaned against the bar, holding his right hand against his head.

'Are yuh ready?' asked Bellew, and Andy nodded.

'Is the number 1256843?' asked Bellew.

Andy looked fixedly at Melancholy. 'No,' he said softly.

'Is it 2549863?'

'No.'

'Is it 9678321?'

Andy fixed Melancholy with a steady stare.

'That's the number.'

'That was jist a dam' lucky guess!' snorted Melancholy.

'Lucky,' grinned Bellew. 'Got any more bettin' moncy?'

Melancholy shook his head, squinting closely at Tolliver, who seemed exhausted by his mental efforts. The bartender gave the money to Bellew, who split it with Tolliver, while Melancholy looked sadly on.

'I'd like to play a game of pool,' said Bellew. Pool was one game Melancholy could not resist.

'I'll play yuh,' he said, and removed his coat, which he hung near the ball-rack.

The game was of little interest to spectators. Tolliver accidentally knocked Melancholy's coat off the hook, but picked it up again and hung it back on the hook. After the game, when the deputy put on his coat, Tolliver was joking him about losing the ten dollars on a simple feat of mind-reading, and shoved Melancholy against the wall rather hard.

Melancholy grabbed for him, but the lanky cowboy stepped quickly away. Melancholy went to the bar with Bellew and had a drink, after which he stood behind some poker players, watching the run of the cards. There was a peculiar odor in the air. The players sniffed, Melancholy sniffed. Where did it come from? And it was not at all pleasant.

'Whatcha got on yuh?' queried one of the players.

'Nothin' on me,' denied Melancholy a bit warmly.

'Well, somebody has. Smells fit for a buzzard.'

'I didn't smell it until I come over here.'

61

'Ask Tolliver,' laughed a player. 'Mebby it's on our minds.'

'I've heard of folks bein' dirty-minded,' said Melancholy, and walked out of the saloon.

He went to his office and sat down to smoke a cigarette. The odor was even stronger over here. He sniffed and sniffed, holding a pack of cigarette papers between thumb and finger.

'I shore can't figure it out,' he told himself, and reached in the right-hand pocket of his coat to get his tobacco. His hand jerked out quickly, the fingers gobby with a yellowish, sticky substance, to which adhered small pieces of eggshell. It was smashed eggs – eggs which had long since passed the prime of life.

Thus it came that Melancholy Day was mad. His coat was now hanging outside, that pocket cut completely out and thrown away along with a package of Durham. The room still stank, and Melancholy had sworn a feud against Bellew and Tolliver. He remembered Tolliver shoving him against the wall.

He went to the door and looked across the street. In the light of the saloon windows he could see two men on the steps. They were Bellew and Tolliver. As he looked at them, they stepped off the sidewalk and started toward the office. Melancholy looked around quickly, looking for a suitable weapon, and his eyes fell upon the office water bucket, full of water. It was not exactly what he wanted, but it would suffice.

Quickly he picked it up, stepped back against the wall near the door, and waited.

'Here's where part of that dam' Doughnut outfit gits a bath,' he grinned grimly. It was quite a large bucket.

He heard footsteps on the gravel of the street, a clump of feet on the wooden sidewalk, a man in the doorway. And then Melancholy threw that big bucket of water full in his face. There came a yelp of surprise, the clatter of loose boards, a man running. Melancholy stepped to the doorway, ready to throw the bucket, but there was no one in sight. A man was running up the street. On the sidewalk was a floppy old straw hat, and between the doorway and the hat was a yellow envelope.

Melancholy picked it up, shook the water off, and looked foolishly at it.

'Telegram,' he said dumbly. 'Whatcha know about that?'

Stepping back into the office, he opened it and looked closely at the writing, which read:

SHERIFF OF CINCO CITY NUMBER SIX HELD UP AND ROBBED NEAR TOP OF TEJUNGA

GRADE AT ABOUT NINE-THIRTY STOP BROKE
TRAIN IN TWO REAR CARS RAN AWAY AND
MADE BAD WRECK AT TEJUNGA STOP TWO
MEN DID JOB BUT NO DESCRIPTION YET
STOP

CARTER
AGENT AT TEJUNGA

'Huh!' grunted Melancholy. 'I reckon I better
find Panamint Pelley.'

By the time he made up his mind on the
matter, Panamint came in.

'Where's my telegram?' he demanded. 'Jist
met the telegraph operator up the street, and
he tells me about somebody tryin' to drown
him down here when he brought a telegram.
What happened?'

'Here's yore danged telegram – and I reckon
he's right. My mistake.'

'Mostly always is,' scanning the telegram.
'Holee smoke! Wrecked the train and robbed
– git the horses quick!'

Panamint Pelley fairly jigged in the middle
of the room.

'You ain't aimin' to chase no robber in the
dark, are yuh, Panamint?'

'Well, what in hell else is there to do?'

'Nothin' definite. We don't know exactly
where they pulled the job. If it was two men,
they prob'ly had their horses staked pretty

64

close, and by this time, they're a long ways from there.'

'Just the same, we're goin'. Git the horses, will yuh? Sa-a-ay, what smells so danged funny around here?'

'I'll git the horses,' said Melancholy quickly. 'Lotta good it'll do, but I'll git 'em.'

He stopped in the doorway and looked back at the sheriff.

'Did you ever hear that Andy Tolliver could read minds?'

'Who's mind did he ever read?'

'Mine.'

'Must be awful quick at it,' grunted Panamint as he stuffed cartridges into the loading-gate of his Winchester.

'Quick?'

'Shore – quick. You can't keep yore mind on anythin' long enough f'r an average mind-reader to git set.'

'Oh!' grunted Melancholy, and went clumping down the sidewalk to the stable.

'What's wrong, Panamint?'

The sheriff looked up quickly. Andy Tolliver and Ward Bellew were in the doorway, grinning sheepishly. They had heard about the telegraph operator getting a bath, which had been intended for them. Panamint considered them gravely for several moments.

65

'Hold up yore right hands,' he said sharply. 'Up – quick!'

Wonderingly they obeyed. In fact, Tolliver put up both hands – and both men complained bitterly when Panamint swore them in as deputies. He told them about the robbery and wreck.

'But they're expectin' us out at the ranch,' objected Bellew.

'And need us bad,' added Tolliver.

'Uncle Billy said that if we wasn't back –'

'Yeah, I know what he said. He said if yuh wasn't back inside a year, the Doughnut outfit would be a lot better off. Go git yore horses, and I'll give yuh each a rifle.'

Still complaining, they went to the hitch-rack. When Melancholy brought their two horses in front of the office and found that Panamint had deputized Bellew and Tolliver, he did a double-shuffle on the sidewalk. Contrary to general belief, no cowboy relishes a long ride, with a possible chance of hot lead at the finish.

'I told Panamint to take you fellers along,' said Melancholy, rubbing it in as much as possible. 'Yore mind-readin' ability will prob'ly help us out a lot. Ward can ask 'em if they're the robbers, while Andy listens to their mind clickin'. This is shore a combination yuh can't beat.'

'Ye-a-ah,' snorted Bellew. 'And when we find the wrong one, yuh can throw a bucket of water in his face.'

'Let's go,' said the sheriff, swinging into his saddle, and they galloped away under the Arizona stars.

'They're prob'ly settin' right there along the track,' said Tolliver, 'with the money in their laps. Train-robbers mostly allus do that.'

'You *can* read minds,' admitted Melancholy. 'I thought the same thing.'

The exact spot of the robbery had not been described in the telegram, but all the men were familiar with the country. It was about six miles from Cinco City to the top of Tejunga grades, but the sheriff did not spare the horses. They were on the down grade, when he swung his horse off the road and over to the right-of-way fence.

'Ought to be along here,' he grunted, as they tied their horses and crawled through the barbed-wire fence.

They climbed up the short, rocky slope, through which ran the railroad cut, and stopped on the top. Fifteen feet below them was the track.

'It shore wasn't done here,' said Melancholy. 'They couldn't climb this bank. We'll have to look farther down, below this deep cut, and mebby –'

'Sh-h-h-h-h!' hissed Panamint. Less than a hundred yards down the track, someone had lit a match.

'Two men, I think,' whispered Tolliver.

'Blew the safe all to hell, and they're lookin' for money,' said the sheriff. 'Git down and we'll sneak in on 'em.'

Came the slither of gravel, a short curse, the sound of a body hitting the slippery shale, and Melancholy Day went over the edge of the cut, flinging his rifle away, as he grabbed for support.

Wham! The rifle went off on impact, and the echoes clattered back from the hills. The sheriff cursed wildly and ran down to the fence, where he got all tangled up in his haste and was obliged to wait until Andy could cut him loose. Then the sheriff surged through between the wires, caught one of the barbs in his leather chaps and fell headlong, almost into his horse, which surged back quickly and snapped off the rotted fence-post.

The snapping and twanging of the wires was too much for the rest of the horses, and a few moments later there were four horses, heading in different directions, dragging fence-posts or sections of barbed wire. The horses belonging to Tolliver and Bellew headed back toward Cinco City, while the other two seemed inclined to visit Tejunga. Within five minutes

Andy and Ward had captured their animals, but they didn't go to the sheriff's assistance.

By mutual consent they struck back toward the Circle Dot Ranch, and were swallowed up in the night. The sheriff didn't go far, and in a few minutes Melancholy Day showed up. He was scratched considerably, and his clothes were torn, but he was able to swear as he came weaving back to the fence where the sheriff met him and told what happened.

'And jist when we had them fellers dead t' rights,' groaned Melancholy.

'Yea-a-a-ah! With you fallin' off the bank and shootin' yore rifle in the air. Dead t' nothin'!'

'I suppose I fell off there on purpose.'

'I dunno,' groaned the sheriff. 'I'm no mind-reader, yuh know.'

'Where's them other two man-hunters?'

'Their broncs headed for Cinco, and it don't take no mind-reader to tell me we've seen the last of 'em for tonight. What'll we do?'

'Well, our horses are headed for Tejunga, and she's a long ways to Cinco in the dark.'

'Well, let's go to Tejunga. Might get more news down there.'

Sad Sontag and Swede Harrigan, crouched behind some mesquite near the road, saw them go past, walking heavily. After they were far down the road, the two cowboys crossed the road, mounted their horses behind a clump of brush, and rode slowly on toward Cinco City.

'Kinda funny,' said Sad musingly. 'I'd like to know who fired that shot, and why these two men are walkin' in the dark. Anyway, there's no use lookin' for the spot where the train was robbed; so our best bet is to find Cinco City and go to bed.'

'I heard horses runnin', before we got out of the cut,' said Swede.

'So did I. It's shore queer all the way around.'

'Been a queer evenin', all the way around, if yuh ask me.'

Clare slept that night at the Tejunga hotel. It was not a first-class hostelry by any manner of means, but she was grateful for a bed. The wrecker arrived, and was busy out there on the tracks trying to get things cleared up and new track laid. Clare wondered what became of the tall, gray-eyed cowboy, who had helped her from the coach, and she also wondered what that other cowboy meant when he said that the Gavins were a tough family. It was evident that the young man's name was Gavin. She decided that he was rather a cool young man, judging by the way

70

he had handled Grover Harris, the drummer. For a long time she was unable to sleep, thinking of their wild ride down the grade, and the terrific crash and flood of dust at the finish.

In the morning Tejunga was normal again. The track had been repaired, the cattle train was gone, and a following passenger train had picked up the wreck-bound crowd.

'Yo're goin' t' Cinco, ain't yuh?' asked the proprietor, as he took Clare to the dining-room.

'Yes, I am.'

'Well, I thought yuh said yuh was last night. There's a train through here in about an hour, and they'll take yuh up.'

'Thank you very much.'

'Yuh don't need t' thank me – it ain't my train.'

Clare smiled, and the old man chuckled at his own joke.

'Did you ever know a man named Cleland?' she asked.

'From Cinco City? Old Million Dollar Cleland? Shore knowed him well. He's in Los Angeles, I reckon. Heard he was, anyway.'

'He's dead.'

'No! Dead? From what did he die?'

Clare explained, while the old man sat down and leaned across the table.

'Shot, eh? Bushed right in the city! Can yuh imagine that? And his body was in that baggage-car last night? Well, I'll be derned!'

He thought it over sadly, while Clare finished breakfast.

'Yuh know why he left this country, don'tcha?' he asked.

'He never told me why.'

The old man explained what he knew about the trouble between the JHC and J Bar 44 outfits, and the killing of Jim Gavin.

'The Gavins would have got him sure, only he went away. It wasn't 'cause the old man was a coward, but he didn't like killin's. He knowed it would drag his own men into the pot, and he didn't want any of 'em hurt. Oh, I can see his p'int in the matter. Them Gavins are a tough outfit, I tell yuh.'

That was the second time the same opinion had been voiced in her hearing.

'And it all started over a little spring of water,' she said slowly.

'Water is the most valuable thing we've got down here, ma'am. Yuh know anythin' about cattle?'

'Not a thing.'

'Uh-huh. Well, yuh'll find a good outfit at the JHC. Ted Bell is foreman. Of course, all I know is what I hear.'

'I see. You spoke about the Gavins – is one of them a young man, with curly hair?'

'Yeah, I believe he has. That's Chuck. And he's as wild as a basket of rattlers. It was his uncle that Cleland killed. Sa-a-ay, I think I seen Chuck here last night. Ain't sure, but I think it was him. Wearin' store clothes.'

'Do you think the Gavins would have killed Mr. Cleland, if he had stayed here in this country?'

'Oh, shore. Of course, the old man would git a few Gavins, too. He wasn't no hunk of piety himself. Funny that somebody would bush him in the city.'

'It was rather queer,' murmured Clare, staring at the none-too-clean tablecloth, as a sudden idea flashed through her mind.

Chuck Gavin had boarded the train in Los Angeles – and the Gavin family hated John Cleland. Perhaps it was only a coincidence. But John Cleland had written at the bottom of his will, 'I no who shot me.'

Clare lifted her eyes and stared at the faded wall-paper.

'Didn't yore breakfast set good?' asked the old man. 'Yuh looked kinda peaked.'

'No, I am all right,' said Clare.

It was difficult for her to link Chuck Gavin with the murder of Cleland; but Chuck Gavin had been in Los Angeles, the Gavins hated

Cleland – and John Cleland knew who shot him. She wondered if Chuck Gavin knew who she was, and why she was coming to Cinco City.

Pima Simpson met Clare at the Cinco depot. She was the only passenger and, except for the depot agent, Pima was the only person on the platform. He came slowly over to her and she smiled at him, but there was no answering smile. Pima had long since made up his mind that he wasn't going to like her.

'You Miss Nolan?' he asked.

'Yes.'

'I'm Pima Simpson. Ted Bell sent me down to git yuh, if yuh wanted to go out to the ranch.'

'Why, yes. You heard about the wreck?'

'Yes'm, we heard about it.'

Clare looked around the bleak little depot.

'What disposition was made of Mr. Cleland's body?' she asked.

Pima shook his head. 'Ain't seen no body, ma'am.'

'Perhaps it hasn't come in from Tejunga.'

'Well, it ain't here.'

Clare walked around to the little ticket-window and spoke to the agent about it. He removed his cap, scratched his head thoughtfully.

'No, ma'am, I ain't seen nothin' of the

74

kind. The express came through early this mornin'. There was a few things for us, but there wasn't no body.'

'That is very queer. I am positive it was on that train.'

'I dunno, except it wasn't on there when it was unloaded here. The messenger was taken off at Tejunga and shipped back. Hurt pretty bad, they tell me. His bunch of waybills must have been blowed to pieces when they shot the safe 'cause we couldn't find anythin'. Mebby that body wasn't shipped on that train, ma'am.'

'That must be the solution,' said Clare. She turned to Pima, who was carrying her valise. 'If you are ready to go to the ranch –'

'Shore, I'm ready.'

But if Clare had really known what that missing body was to mean to her, she wouldn't have taken its loss so easily.

CHAPTER V

Pima led the way to a buckboard to which was hitched a pair of wild-looking roans, which eyed Pima with evident disfavor. He packed the grips in the rear and motioned Clare to a seat. With a sudden lurch the team swept away from the hitch-rack, and went galloping up the main street, while Clare clung to the seat with one hand and to her hat with the other.

Pima pulled his sombrero low over his eyes and drove the running team with a steady hand. But the sandy road was a bit heavy for speed, and the team slowed to a trot a mile from town. Pima glanced at Clare. Her cheeks were flushed and there was a smile on her lips. Pima snorted to himself. He thought she would be frightened.

'You goin' to run the JHC ranch?' he asked her.

'Why, I don't know. Perhaps I shall. You see, it was given to me by Mr. Cleland.'

'That's what we heard.'

Pima looked keenly at her for a few moments.

'Was you goin' to marry the old man?' he asked.

Clare looked at him wonderingly, not understanding his question.

'Marry him?'

'He willed yuh everythin', yuh know.'

Clare shook her head. 'Why, he was old enough to be my grandfather. Really, I don't know why he left everything to me. In fact, I didn't know he had anything, until after

76

he was dead. To me he was just a likeable old man.'

'Uh-huh. Well' – Pima rubbed his stubbled chin – 'I dunno. Queer about his gittin' killed thataway.'

'He knew who killed him.'

'No! He did? Why didn't he tell?'

'Who knows why? He wrote on the will, "I know who shot me," but no name of the murderer.'

'The old son-of-a-gun! He didn't know he was dyin'. Wanted to pay it back himself. Yeah, that's like Old Million Dollar. An eye for an eye, but he wanted to do the tooth-pullin' for himself. Yeah, that'd be him. Well, there's the old JHC Ranch, ma'am.'

They came around the point of a hill above the ranch buildings, and Clare saw the ranch she had inherited. The main ranch-house was a squatty, two-story affair, about sixty feet long, a mixture of Mexican, Hopi, and American architecture. Behind this building was a patio about eighty feet square, with a thick adobe wall, enclosing the bunk-house and a large storeroom. Behind the patio were the stables and corrals.

A huge arched gate led into the patio from one end of the ranch-house, and another arched gate led to the stables. The patio was flagged with flat stones and in the center were

77

the well and watering-troughs. The old adobe was picturesque, with its tints of white, yellow and red, and a huge live-oak, just inside the west wall, shaded much of the patio. There was a huge porch, and a gourd dipper beside the sweating olla. A few climbing roses, badly neglected, straggled over the railing.

Pima drove to the center of the patio, and the horses nuzzled at the trough, while Clare dismounted and Pima removed the bags. Old Elastic Jones stood in the doorway, red of face, a flour sack draped around his middle, a smear of flour across his cheek. Elastic was baking bread, and he was usually in a bad humor at those times. Clare smiled at him, and he grunted softly. He was all prepared to dislike her, but that smile was disarming, and he found himself grinning back at her.

'Ma'am,' said Pima seriously, 'this here is Elastic Jones, the best cook between the two Poles. Elastic, meet Miss Nolan.'

Clare offered her hand and Elastic took it gingerly.

'Pleased to meetcha, ma'am. Bakin' bread t'day.'

'I can smell it,' she smiled.

Elastic looked her over curiously. 'Wreck didn't hurt yuh none, did it?'

'No, I was very fortunate.'

'Uh-huh. Well, come on in. We ain't got

much to offer a lady around here. Yuh see, we ain't used to ladies on the JHC. I was tellin' Ted we better primp up a little. He's out with the boys and won't be back till supper-time. He didn't say what room to put yuh in. Fact is, he didn't think you'd want to stay out here.'

'I hope I'm not intruding.'

'No, ma'am,' said Pima quickly. 'You ain't protrudin' a-tall. There's plenty room. We'll jist leave yore valises here in the big room, and wait'll Ted gits back. He's foreman, yuh know.'

'Where's the remains of Million Dollar?' asked Elastic.

'They ain't here yet,' replied Pima. 'Prob'ly be in on another train.'

'Jist make yourself at home,' said Elastic. 'I've got to watch the bread.'

Pima went out to take care of the team, and Clare wandered around, looking the place over. It was strictly a man's place. Over the fireplace hung a crayon enlargement of John Cleland; a terrible likeness, with one eye slightly off center and a menacing scowl. Much of the gilt was missing from the ornate frame. The mantel was littered with loose cartridges, cigarette papers, tobacco, and several odd pipes. The table was piled with old magazines, newspapers, and in the center of the room was a pair of boots, standing there bravely, as though the owner had just stepped out of them.

On another wall was an elk head; a terrible example of taxidermy. The lips held a simpering grin and the eyes bulged. One ear had been broken, and hung down rakishly. The floor was colorful with Navajo rugs, which needed cleaning, and the rough floor held numerous cigarette butts.

Elastic shoved his head around the corner of the doorway.

'Oh, you'll find plenty dirt,' he grinned. 'I should have swamped the place out t'day, but I had that dam' bread to bake. Anyway, Ted didn't think you'd come out here. Yuh see, we heard that Million Dollar Cleland had died and left this here ranch to a woman, but – well, it *was* kinda funny.'

'What was funny about it?' asked Clare.

'Well, he never was no hand with wimmin around here.'

'But I have the will,' smiled Clare.

'Yeah, I know. Yuh can't dispute them kinda things. As far as I'm concerned, it don't make me no never mind, but the rest of the boys ain't favorin' no woman boss.'

'Why do they call you Elastic?' asked Clare.

'On account of me stretchin' the truth so far, I reckon.'

80

Elastic hurried back to his oven, and Clare leaned back in an easy-chair. It was evident that she was not at all welcome at the JHC. They didn't want a woman boss. Clare smiled at the idea of her bossing the ranch, when she didn't know the first thing about cattle. It was so warm in the house that she went out on the big porch in the patio, and in a few minutes Elastic came out. The bread was baked. He sat down on the steps and filled his pipe.

'Do you know the Gavin family?' asked Clare.

Elastic snorted angrily. 'Know em? Basket of snakes!'

'It may sound a little strange to you, but Mr. Cleland never told me anything about the trouble between this ranch and the Gavin family. A man in Tejunga told me a little about it, but perhaps you can tell me more about it.'

Elastic sucked thoughtfully on his pipe. It was a big moment in his life. Someone asking him to tell the story of JHC versus J Bar 44. Elastic shut one eye, as he groped for a starting-point.

'Well, it was like this, ma'am –'

At this point Ted Bell rode into the patio, with Larry Delago and Mose Heilman. Elastic swore under his breath, and got slowly to his feet. The three men dismounted near the well, and Bell handed his reins to Delago. Bell had merely given Clare a quick glance, Heilman ignored her entirely, but Delago stared at her with a look of insolent admiration, his lips parted in a white-toothed smile. Heilman turned and walked to the bunk-house, while Delago led the three horses out through the rear archway, glancing back at Clare, as he walked away.

Ted Bell came slowly over to the porch, carrying his sombrero in his hand.

'Ted, this is Miss Nolan,' said Elastic shortly.

'How do you do, Miss Nolan,' said Ted coldly. He didn't offer to shake hands.

'Quite well, thank you.'

'I guess yuh didn't get hurt much in that wreck, didja?'

'Oh, no. It was quite a shock, but we were all very fortunate.'

'Uh-huh,' he turned to Elastic. 'Didja fix Miss Nolan up with a room?'

'Didn't know where yuh wanted to put her, Ted; so I left it to you.'

'Give her the old man's room. Better kick some of the dirt out of it.'

'All right.'

'What arrangements have been made for the funeral?' asked Clare.

Bell sat down on the steps and drew out his cigarette material.

'The coroner will take charge of the body and handle the funeral. He's the undertaker, yuh know. I'll go down and have a talk with him this evenin'.'

'It must have been a blow to you boys. Mr. Cleland was well liked, I believe.'

'Yeah, he was.'

Ted lighted his cigarette, leaned back against the steps and looked at Clare.

'We've all been wonderin' what you'd look like, Miss Nolan. I reckon we've all been wrong. Yuh see, we looked for – well, we couldn't quite figure out what kind of a looker yuh'd be. Million Dollar Cleland wasn't much of a hand with women, but I suppose he's like a lot of men. When they get old – some pretty girl winds him around her finger, and then –'

'That is both unkind and untrue,' said Clare quickly. 'No gentleman –'

'I'm not a gentleman. Do yuh mean to try and convince us that old man Cleland picked yuh out of the blue sky as his heiress?'

'No, I don't think you are a gentleman,' said Clare coldly, 'and I am not going to explain anything. But nothing alters the fact that Mr. Cleland willed me this ranch.'

Ted smiled grimly. 'No, I reckon that's

true enough. Yuh won't want me here when yuh take charge, but I'll run the ranch until the court turns the property over to yuh.'

'Meaning that I am not welcome here now?'

'Stay if yuh want to.'

Larry Delago came back from the stables, swaggering across the patio, a tall, colorful figure. He wore a blue silk shirt and a vermilion handkerchief around his throat. He came up to the porch, and Ted Bell performed the introduction, without getting to his feet.

'*Bienvenido, Señorita,*' smiled Delago, holding out a slim, muscular hand.

Clare shook hands with him, and it seemed to her that the pressure of his hand was unnecessarily severe. At a distance he had been rather a romantic person, but at close range he seemed tawdry, unclean, his dark eyes, almost green in that light, with red flecks like bloodstones.

'We were all wrong, Ted,' he said, without a trace of Spanish accent. 'We pictured a cactus, and we find a yucca; a tall, white yucca, which the Spanish-speaking people call "God's candlesticks." '

Clare flushed, and it seemed to amuse Delago.

'Drop it,' growled Bell, and Delago laughed at him.

'I suppose Pima Simpson can take me back to Cinco City,' said Clare.

'Yo're not goin' back there, are yuh?' asked Delago quickly, lapsing into the cowboy vernacular.

'I reckon she'd be better satisfied – for the present,' replied Ted.

'Much better,' added Clare firmly.

Delago looked curiously at Ted, but said nothing.

Ted lost no time in ordering Pima Simpson to hitch up and take Clare back to Cinco City. The old man seemed a little disappointed, but not surprised, as he confided to Clare on their return journey.

'Ted never was no hand with the wimmin, and when yuh come right down to it, the JHC ain't no place for a woman. Larry didn't like it. Yuh see, he's what you'd call a lady-killer, he is.'

'I presume Larry is Mr. Delago.'

'That's him. Says he's half Spanish. Spanish – hell! Puts on colors till he looks like a danged Fourth-of-July parade. But he's a good puncher. One of the best riders in this country. Uh-huh. I expect there'll be a big funeral for John Cleland. Ought to be. Everybody'll come except the Gavin family. But yuh can't expect 'em to be there.'

'One of them came on the same car with me

from Los Angeles,' said Clare.

'Yea-a-a-ah?'

'I think they call him Chuck.'

'Well, great lovely dove! Are yuh shore it was Chuck?'

Clare described him fairly well, and the old man nodded.

'That's him all right. Ah-ha-a-a-ah! Well, well!'

Clare wondered at the explosive exclamations, but the old man offered no explanations. He took her to the Cinco City Hotel, where she signed the little register and was given a room. It was a little better than the one at Tejunga. At least she could be comfortable until a change could be made.

The sheriff's office had been a busy place that day. Panamint and Melancholy were out at daylight, trying to find the spot where the holdup had been made; failing in this, they had circled the hills, trying to pick out some sort of a clue, only to come back to Cinco City and admit that they had found nothing. There were plenty of telegrams from the express company, and it seemed that something like eighteen thousand dollars was missing. The latest wire advised them that a company detective was on his way to Cinco City.

'And may Gawd give him second sight,' said Panamint.

'And sense enough to keep it to himself,' added Melancholy, still reacting to the loss of that ten dollars.

It was a little later in the morning that the stable keeper told Melancholy about the two strangers who had ridden in and stabled their horses in the middle of the night. He showed the deputy a tall blue-roan and a short bay, munching away at their oats. Melancholy looked at the brands, examining the two saddles, which were hanging up behind the stalls, and went back to report it to Panamint.

Panamint was interested. Under the circumstances, two strange riders, coming to town in the middle of the night, were worth an investigation; so he and Melancholy went on a still hunt and found the two strangers playing pool at the Cinco City Bar.

'Couple of forked gents,' observed Melancholy, as he and the sheriff stood at the bar, his sad eyes following the two players. 'Want to ask 'em questions, Panamint?'

'What in hell would I ask 'em – if they robbed the train?'

'Ask 'em where they came from and what –'

'And have 'em tell me where I could go, eh?'

'Yea-a-ah, prob'ly. Well, I dunno. Mebbe they'll talk.'

Sontag and Harrigan finished their game and came over to the bar, where the sheriff eyed them speculatively, but said nothing, until Sad, happening to notice the star on the sheriff's vest, asked him if he had caught the robbers.

'Not yet,' said Panamint grimly. He meant to be severe, but melted under Sad's broad grin.

'Wonderin' who we are, ain'tcha?' asked Sad.

'Wonderin' – not askin'.'

'Fit to be a sheriff,' grinned Sad. 'I'll buy a drink.'

'Oh, all right.'

'Deputy included,' said Sad. Melancholy affected a yawn, stepped up to the bar and squinted at the array of bottles on the back-bar.

'What was that soft drink I had?'

'Gin,' smiled the bartender.

'That's mine.'

'We're waitin' for the railroad detectives,' confided the sheriff. 'They'll come and look around, admit that robbery has been done, and then go back.'

'I suppose,' smiled Sad. 'Do yuh know Buck Hogan?'

'Sawbuck outfit? I shore do,' said the sheriff warmly.

'We were with Buck down at Tejunga, when the wreck occurred last night. In fact, we were intendin' to work on his ranch in the Sweetwater.'

'We seen that cow train go through. So that was Buck Hogan, eh?' The sheriff was curious.

'How did it happen yuh didn't go to Sweetwater?'

'Changed our minds at the last moment.'

'Uh-huh,' replied the sheriff, unconvinced.

A man came in past the bar, spurs rattling, chaps creaking. It was Tom Hawker, of the Tomahawk outfit. He nodded to the sheriff and went on toward the rear of the room, where four men were playing a game of seven-up. Sontag's eyes followed the tall cowman's back, the broad muscular shoulders, narrow waist, narrow hips, long legs, encased in bat-wing chaps, a holstered gun swinging low on his right thigh.

Hawker talked for a few moments with one of the men, and came back past the bar. His deep-set eyes, hidden beneath heavy brows, seemed to look sharply at Sad Sontag as he went past. Sad squinted thoughtfully, wondering where he had seen this man before.

'High cheek-bones, bushy brows, and a bulldog jaw,' he enumerated to himself. The sheriff was talking with Swede when Sad

89

interrupted them with, 'What's that man's name, sheriff?'

'Tom Hawker. He owns the Tomahawk outfit.'

'Tom Hawker?'

'Yeah.'

The name meant nothing to Sad – but the man did. Somewhere in his wanderings he had known such a man, but he was not called Hawker. Sad searched his memory deeply.

'Known him long?' asked Sad.

'Prob'ly three years. Bought out a feller named Crane, registered the Tomahawk iron and built up a nice herd. His brother Pete and a couple of Injun breeds work for him. Tom is a nice feller.'

'Looks all right.'

'Oh, shore. Good cowman, too.'

The sheriff looked at his watch. 'Train about due, and I've got to meet them railroad detectives. Lot of good they'll do. We can't even locate the place where the holdup was pulled off. Last night we went down there, took a coupla Circle Dot punchers with us, and tried to find the place – but didn't.'

'Tell 'em the rest of it,' growled Melancholy. 'Tell 'em that we seen a couple of men lightin' matches on the railroad track, and I fell off the bank and fired my gun. And then tell 'em how you got stuck in the barbed-wire fence and scared the horses so bad that they busted away from us and we had to walk plump to Tejunga before we caught 'em.'

'That,' said the sheriff severely, 'is nobody's dam' business.'

'No,' admitted Melancholy, 'but it completes the story.'

Sad and Swede grinned at each other, after the sheriff had left the saloon with his deputy. Melancholy had explained the mystery of the shot in the dark and of the two men walking down the road. They crossed the street and sat down in the shade.

'I'm glad he fell off that bank,' laughed Sad. 'It shore saved us a lot of explainin'. I reckon the sheriff still suspects us of something'.'

'Prob'ly; sheriffs usually do.'

They were lounging in the shade, when Pima brought Clare to the hotel. Sad recognized her as being the girl he had helped from the wreck. The train came in, and the sheriff brought the two railroad detectives to his office for a conference. Melancholy left the office and came up to Sad and Swede, where he sprawled in the shade and rolled a smoke.

'Nothin' left for you fellers to do, I suppose,' observed Swede.

Melancholy grinned sadly. 'I reckon not. Them two fellers shore came loaded with questions that nobody can answer. Hell! If we could answer all them questions, we wouldn't be county officers.'

'Lookin' at it from your viewpoint, who might have pulled the job?' asked Sad.

'*Quien sabe?* There's no clue to work on. Any two men in the country might have done it. Somebody shore has got plenty money t'day. Bimeby they'll drift out where they can spent it, I s'pose.'

'I just saw a man and a woman drive in in a buckboard. The woman is young and mighty good-lookin'. I seen her last night at the wreck.'

'Yeah, I seen 'em come in. The man is Pima Simpson, one of the JHC punchers, and the woman's name is Nolan. She inherited the JHC. I ain't had a good look at her, but I know she's the one. Old Million Dollar Cleland was killed in Los Angeles, and he willed her the ranch and everythin' else he owned. They tell me she was bringin' the old man's body back to here to bury it, but I've been too busy to hear much about what's bein' done.'

'Yuh say he was killed in Los Angeles?'

'Murdered, they tell me. Yessir, bushed right in a city.'

Sad Sontag slowly rolled a cigarette, a quizzical expression in his eyes.

'What else do yuh know about Cleland?' he asked.

'Quite a lot – up to the time he left here.'

And Melancholy Day gave them a description of what had happened between the JHC and the J Bar 44, when John Cleland killed Jim Gavin in the Cinco City Bar. Melancholy was a born story-teller, and when he finished, Sontag and Harrigan knew the local history of the Cinco range almost as well as the people of the range did.

CHAPTER VI

Shortly after Melancholy had finished his tale, a man came along the sidewalk near them. He was a man past middle age, slightly gray, walking with a decided limp. He nodded pleasantly to the deputy.

'Hiya, Doc,' said Melancholy. 'Did the old man's body git in all right?'

'Not yet,' replied the man gravely. 'I understood it was to have been on that train last night, but it was not. There has been two trains through here since then, but the body has not arrived. Possibly it will be in this afternoon. No arrangements have been made for the funeral; so the delay will not make so much difference.'

The man walked on, and Melancholy told them that the man was Doctor Holman, who was also undertaker and coroner.

'I didn't know you fellers, so I couldn't introduce yuh,' he grinned. 'My name's Day – Melancholy Day. There used to be a puncher around here who recited poetry quite a lot, and one evenin' I went into the Cinco Saloon, and he says, "The melancholy days are here, the saddest of the year." I'd been sufferin' from a bad tooth, and I reckon I did look sad. Anyway, that name stuck to me.'

Sad introduced himself and Swede to the deputy, and they shook hands solemnly.

'Look who's comin',' whispered Swede.

Clare had left the hotel and was coming down the sidewalk toward them. Sad got to his feet and stood on the edge of the sidewalk. Clare recognized him and they smiled at each other.

'Feelin' all right today, ma'am?' he asked.

'Just fine, thank you. Do you live here?'

'Temporarily.'

'Oh, I see. I was on my way to the depot, seeking a little information.'

'Mind if I walk down with you?'

'I wish you would.'

They went away together, and Swede grinned widely.

'Somethin' has gone wrong with Sad,' he declared.

'It comes to every man,' said the deputy gravely, 'and lookin' at her, I don't blame him. We might kill a little time with a game of pool.'

'Suits me jist right; c'mon.'

Clare wanted to talk with someone and she soon found that Sad was a good listener. They went to the depot, where Clare inquired about the body of John Cleland. The agent knew nothing about it, and didn't seem to care much, but did agree to send out a tracer. Clare showed him the ticket she had been obliged to buy for the shipment of the body, and he agreed that someone had made a mistake.

Sad explained that it might be a costly mistake for the express company, and the man seemed more impressed. A package was a package to him, but this was the body of a dead man.

'I'll find it for yuh, lady,' he said gravely. 'A full-grown man in a wooden overcoat ain't so small that it could get misplaced. Don't you worry.'

Sad walked back to the hotel with Clare,

and she told him some of her story; how she met John Cleland, thinking all the while that he was a poor old man, barely getting along. She showed Sad the will and he studied it carefully. It was a tragic little document, and there were tears in her eyes as she told him how the old man had written that will. The letters were a scrawl, but the signature showed he had steeled his nerves to make a perfect signature.

'I don't reckon any court would dispute that document,' said Sad. 'Have yuh been out to the ranch?'

Clare folded the paper and put it in her pocket-book.

'Yes, but I don't believe I was welcome out there; so I came back here to stay until after the will is probated.'

'Selected a lawyer yet?'

'No, I haven't. I will in –'

'Wait a few days, will yuh? I reckon the first thing to do is to go up to the county clerk and get that recorded. I don't say everythin' ain't right, but yuh can't afford to make a slip.'

'Why, you do not suppose anybody would try to get it from me, do you?'

'Somebody murdered John Cleland.'

'Are you trying to frighten me?'

'No, ma'am.'

'Do you know anything about the Gavin family?'

'Only what I've heard since I came here. They evidently hated Cleland, and there's been sort of an enmity between the JHC and the Gavin outfit ever since Cleland killed Jim Gavin.'

'I suppose the Gavins will hate me, too.'

'Well,' smiled Sad, 'they hadn't ought to hate *you*.'

'I don't want anybody to hate me,' wistfully.

Leaving Sad at the hotel, she went to the bank, where she introduced herself to Frank Welden. She didn't know he was a brother of Harold Welden, even after he told her his name. There was very little resemblance.

'I heard about you inheriting the JHC,' he told her pleasantly. 'Quite a handful for a girl to handle, don't you think?'

'I don't know a thing about cattle. I feel that I need a lawyer, and I wondered if you could recommend one.'

'Why – yes, I can. You're staying at the hotel? I'll send one down to see you this evening, a Charley Tolman. He handles some legal work for the bank, and we think a lot of his ability. I understand you brought Cleland's body back here with you.'

'That is what I thought,' said Clare gravely,

97

'but it isn't here. The man at the depot is tracing it now.'

'You were in that wreck?'

'Yes.'

'Came near being a serious thing, I understand.'

'It was a terrible shock, but we were all very fortunate, I think.'

'Very.'

'And you will send Mr. Tolman down to see me this evening?'

'Right after supper, Miss Nolan. If there is anything else I can do for you, don't hesitate to ask me. Remember, you belong to Cinco City, now.'

'Thank you very much, and it is kind of you to say that. I have felt – well, an outsider.'

'I understand. You are from the city – and our ways are different. But you will fit in. We're not as rough as we have been painted.'

After Clare left the bank, Frank Welden sat down at his desk, leaned back and lighted a cigar, clamping it tight with his lean jaw, while his keen eyes closed behind his glasses.

'So that's the girl Hal was stuck on, eh?' he muttered to himself. 'Don't blame him. Good-looking and may have brains. Hate to disappoint her, but she will soon find out the shape of her inheritance. I'll have

Charley tell her about it; he loves bad news for other people.'

The Cinco range was well represented at the Cinco Saloon that night, and Sad had an opportunity to study the men from different outfits. Melancholy pointed out Tom Hawker and his brother, Pete. Sad was sure he had never seen Pete before, but wasn't quite so sure about Tom.

Melancholy pointed out Ted Bell, foreman of the JHC, and old Bat Gavin, head of the J Bar 44. Gavin was a huge man, gaunt, bearded, slightly stooped, hard of features. With him were Dick Ellers and Dan McKenna. Larry Delago and Mose Heilman were with Ted Bell. Delago was inclined to be boisterous, and Sad tabulated him as a show-off. Ward Bellew and Andy Tolliver came in from the Circle Dot. They grinned widely at Melancholy, who snorted disgustedly.

'They won ten dollars off me on a mind-readin' deal,' he told Sad. 'That danged Andy Tolliver shore can read minds.'

Sad was interested and amused when Melancholy explained what had been done. The two men had stopped to talk with Tom Hawker, who was sitting on the edge of a poker table, showing them how to palm a playing card. It was a simple trick, used by magicians and card artists, but difficult to do, except through much practice.

Sad's eyes grew thoughtful, as he watched Hawker palm the card, and back in his memory grew a scene. It was a crowded hall in a mining camp. It was a rough hall, with a small stage, and on this stage was a magician, enthralling that rough crowd with his feats of legerdemain. The hall was packed with humanity, laughing, applauding.

Tomorrow would be payday, and they were making merry in anticipation of a big time. That magician was Tom Hawker, younger, dressed differently. Sad was sure of that face now. He remembered what happened next morning. The paymaster was found dead, the payroll gone. He had been murdered – knifed – early in the evening. By the time an investigation was started, the magician and his two assistants had disappeared and never were apprehended, although a wide search had been made.

And here was the same man, no longer a magician, but a respected cattleman. Sad wondered if Hawker was really going straight. He could not remember what his assistants had looked like.

'Kinda slick with them cards, eh?' said Melancholy.

'That takes a lot of practice,' replied Sad.

Andy Tolliver was trying to do it, but his fingers were too clumsy.

'He can shore read minds,' sighed Melancholy.

'That was a simple trick,' explained Sad. 'The number was selected. Tolliver and Bellew had agreed that the third number asked would be the right one. All Bellew had to do was to name two sets of numbers, which were wrong, and then to name the right one. If Bellew didn't know the right number, it's a cinch Tolliver would never be able to call it. They had it all set to take yore money, and you paid for the experiment.'

'My Gawd!' grunted Melancholy. 'I've a notion to kill both of 'em.'

Later that evening the sheriff told Sad that the detectives had gone down to Tejunga on a freight train.

'Did they find out anythin'?' asked Sad.

'Oh, shore; they found out that I didn't know anythin'. Pretty soon they'll find out that they don't know anythin' – and go back home.'

The next morning Sontag met Clare and her attorney on the street. Tolman was a man of about thirty-five, blond, weak-eyed, and not very strong physically. They were coming from the depot when Sad met them, and as

Clare did not know Sad's name, introductions were waived temporarily.

'We have been trying to locate the body,' she said. 'Isn't it queer that nobody knows where it went? Mr. Tolman sent a telegram to a lawyer down in Los Angeles, asking for more definite information. The depot agent here has a number of telegrams regarding it, and they say the body was shipped on Number Six, the train which was wrecked. But it certainly was not on that train, when it arrived here. You see, the express car was not wrecked.'

'Miss Nolan is in a peculiar predicament,' explained the lawyer. 'Unless this Los Angeles lawyer, who it seems has known the deceased for a number of years, can positively swear to the identity of the corpse, it will be difficult to prove that John Cleland is dead. *Corpus delicti*, you understand.'

Sad smiled slowly at the lawyer. 'Yeah, that makes it tough. But how about other folks who have known him in Los Angeles? Couldn't this lady swear to the identity?'

'Not very well. You see, she is his beneficiary. And as far as that is concerned, she has no proof that the man she knew was John Cleland of Cinco City.'

'How about his signature on that will?'

'That is a possibility. His signature must

102

be on that mortgage at the bank, but until the signatures are compared, I am unable to make any statement. However, we hope for a favorable reply from this attorney.'

'You say there is a mortgage at the bank?' said Clare.

'Oh, yes. I do not know the amount, but it is considerable. Most of the cattlemen have mortgages, you see. You can find out the amount from Mr. Welden at the bank.'

'Isn't it queer that the banker should have the same name as that of the Los Angeles lawyer?' said Clare thoughtfully.

'Not so queer, when you know they are brothers.'

'Not really?'

'Oh, yes. Harold has never been out here, but they keep in touch with each other all the time.'

'Well, that really is strange,' said Clare. 'Harold Welden never mentioned having a brother out here.'

'Strange things happen in Arizona,' smiled Sad.

'Arizona is no different from any other State,' said the lawyer quickly.

'No-o-o-o, that's true. Well, I hope everythin' turns out right, Miss Nolan. I figure it will. If yo're entitled to that property, nothin' can stop yuh from gettin' it. Somebody may put a lot of bumps and ruts in yore road, but yuh'll ride over 'em.'

'I hope so, Mr. – er –'

'Sontag, ma'am. Mostly called Sad.'

'Oh, yes – Mr. Sontag. This is Mr. Tolman who is handling this case for me.'

Tolman did not offer to shake hands, merely nodding, and they walked on.

Sad went to the sheriff's office, where he found Panamint Pelley.

'You didn't find the spot where that holdup was pulled off, didja?' asked Sad.

'Never found nothin'.'

'Suppose we go and look for it.'

The sheriff looked intently at Sad.

'What for?'

'The body of John Cleland was shipped on the express car, and was in that car when it was held up.'

'Yeah? What about it?'

'Yuh know, the body never got here.'

Panamint squinted queerly at Sad. 'Yuh don't mean to say that somebody stole that body, do yuh?'

'It never arrived here.'

'Well, what in hell would anybody steal a corpse for?'

'Reasons don't make any difference – the body was stolen.'

The sheriff considered it thoughtfully.

104

Finally he shut one eye, looked at Sad, and drawled slowly, 'Who in hell are you, anyway, I'd like to know?'

'You know my name, don'tcha?'

'Yeah – Sontag; but that don't mean anythin' to me.'

'That's fine. Now we understand each other perfectly, and yuh might as well get yore horse, 'cause I'm goin' anyway.'

'Well, I'll be – oh, all right.'

The sheriff went out to his stable, mumbling to himself. Who was this Sontag to order him around? 'Understand each other perfectly, eh? Talks crazy. Who would steal a corpse from a train, anyway? No sense in it. Got to humor crazy people, I suppose. But who gave him the right to order the sheriff around? Shore tell him about it, y'betcha.'

He mounted his horse and met Sontag in front of the livery stable.

'Glad yuh mentioned about goin' down there,' said the sheriff. 'I'd shore like to find the exact spot.'

They had nothing to direct them, except the engineer's statement that the robbery had been done near the top of the Tejunga grade; so they followed the right-of-way fence from the top of the grade, looking for a possible break in the barbed wires, but found none. Riding back to the top, they tied their horses

105

to the fence and walked down the track. Panamint showed Sad where Melancholy had fallen off the bank and accidentally fired his rifle.

About a hundred yards farther down the grade, Sad found the wrapper from a small express package, which had been blown apart. It had been blown into a thorny bush at the top of the cut. There were heel-marks in the dirt along the track. A hundred feet below this spot the track crossed a small ravine over a box culvert.

Here they found more heel-tracks, apparently heading up this ravine, and, after climbing the fence again, they found wheel-tracks where a vehicle had been off the road and near the fence. The ground was so hard they were unable to determine which way the vehicle had headed, after leaving the railroad. Neither were the horse-tracks plain. A certain amount of travel along that old highway had blotted out any chance of trailing them.

'First time I ever heard of a robber usin' a wagon,' said the sheriff, as he studied the tire marks.

'Probably the first time yuh ever heard of a robber stealin' a corpse, too,' grinned Sad.

'That's right; they'd have to use a wagon.'

There was nothing further to be done; so they went back to Cinco City. Sad was curious to know what word the lawyer had received from Los Angeles. He found Clare in the lobby of the hotel, talking with Tolman. She handed Sad the telegram to Tolman, which read:

WIRE RECEIVED AND CAN SAY I AM NOT POSITIVE MURDERED MAN WAS J. H. CLELAND AS I DID NOT EXAMINE BODY
HAROLD WELDEN

Sad gave her the telegram and turned to Tolman.

'You are Miss Nolan's attorney?'

'Yes,' crisply.

'All right; here's somethin' to think about. The men who robbed the express car stole the body of J. H. Cleland.'

'Why – why, that's ridiculous!'

'My heavens, why would they do that?' gasped Clare.

Sad smiled slowly. 'Not so ridiculous, after all. Remember that old-time Chinese laundry saying – no tickee, no washee? Fits this case exactly. No corpse, no inheritance. The Los Angeles lawyer was unable to positively identify the body. That was Miss Nolan's sole chance to prove it was Cleland, unless the signature proves it. Find the man who would profit by not having any will.'

107

Clare shook her head sadly. 'Mr. Tolman compared the signatures, and they are not alike. I'm afraid – well' – she shook her head bravely – 'it is something I have never had; so I can't lose, can I?'

'That's the spirit,' applauded Sad, 'but don't weaken.'

'I am not going to weaken. In stealing the body, they admit it was the body of John Cleland. I'm not sure that Harold Welden did look closely at the body that night. Perhaps he merely took it for granted. It was on the floor when the police talked with him, but he did not examine it. When they saw my name on that will, they sent for me right away, and Harold Welden came a little later. Oh, I wish Mr. Cleland had told who shot him.'

'Too bad he didn't,' agreed Sad.

'What is your interest in this matter,' queried the lawyer.

Sad smiled slowly. 'If I wanted yuh to know, I would have told yuh without yuh askin' me, Mr. Tolman.'

'Oh, I see,' said Tolman blankly. He turned to Clare. 'I guess this is all we can do until something new turns up, Miss Nolan.'

'It seems that way,' agreed Clare, and the lawyer went out.

'Have you still got that will?' asked Sad.

'Yes, I still have it.'

'Good. If you'd trust me with it, I'd like to lock that up in the sheriff's safe. It's all you've got to prove anythin' with, yuh know.'

'Why, I – I suppose it would be all right. Mr. Tolman –'

'He wouldn't approve,' smiled Sad. 'Lawyers always object to everythin'. But this' – Sad hesitated – 'is different. I'd bet my socks that the sheriff is on the square, but I wouldn't gamble on anybody else I've met.'

Clare handed him the will, dubiously, perhaps, because she wasn't sure it was the proper thing to do, and looked a bit anxiously after him as he went down the wooden sidewalk to the sheriff's office, where he sealed it in an envelope and had the sheriff put it in his safe. He did not tell the sheriff what it contained, but that it was valuable.

He found Swede at the Cinco Saloon, playing pool with Melancholy Day, and after the game he told Swede what he and the sheriff had discovered. Swede was rather amazed.

'That's shore a queer deal,' he said. 'Who would profit by stealin' that old man's carcass?'

'That's the big question. The J Bar 44 want that water, and if the girl gets the ranch, she can't sell it to the Gavin outfit, even if she wanted to. If they were foolish enough to pull off this deal, they've shore pulled off a criminal act, without any chance of profit to themselves.'

Swede grinned slowly and shook his head.

'Why not drop this deal, Sad? Cinco City don't mean anythin' to me and you. Let's pull down in the Sweetwater country and go to work.'

Sad sat down on the edge of the sidewalk and rolled a smoke. There was a lot of truth in Swede's argument. Cinco City meant nothing to them. There was nothing in it for Sad to puzzle his brain over these things. They would be much better off working for Buck Hogan at the Sawbuck Ranch.

Sad was not a detective, but he had cleared up a few range mysteries, and had gained quite a reputation in the Sundown country. He possessed a keen mind, and since he had been big enough to make his own way in the world he had always done more or less fighting for the underdog.

Christened James J. by his parents, he soon, on account of his long face and usually somber eyes, acquired the nick-name of 'Sad.' On his way to the Sundown country he had fallen in with Michael M. Harrigan, better known as 'Swede,' and since that time they were inseparable. Swede was a top-hand cowboy, with an overdeveloped sense of humor and unlimited nerve.

Together they had cleaned up the outlaw element of the Sundown country, and kept it clean. Then Sad got married, and, as Swede expressed it, 'broke the set,' but Sad's wife hungered for the city, went away on a visit to some relatives, and decided not to come back. Sad sold the TJ outfit, gave her the proceeds, and started roaming, along with Swede, who sold out his horse ranch and went along.

The Cattle Association tried to hire Sad as a range detective, but he refused; not that he feared his own ability to make good, but because he wanted to be free to follow his nose, just as he was doing now.

They had little money left – and plenty of time. Swede sat there and looked sideways at Sad, knowing that Sad would not quit the case.

'You ain't stuck on that girl, are yuh?' asked Swede, as they prepared for bed that night.

'I ain't stuck on no girl,' thoughtfully. 'I've proved that a ramblin' cowboy ain't got no right to marry. It ain't a square deal for the woman – nor for the man, as far as that goes. I've jist been thinkin' of somethin', and I want you to kinda concentrate on what I'm tellin' yuh. Do you remember the time we was

111

up in Colorado – Terryville, I reckon it was – a minin' camp?'

'Shore, I remember. Five years ago. Somebody killed the paymaster up there.'

'That's the place and the time. Remember that show in the big hall and –'

'That magician? He was supposed to have been one of the gang, wasn't he?'

'Didja get a good look at Tom Hawker?'

'That lantern-jawed owner of the Tomahawk?'

Swede blinked thoughtfully, trying to hook the toe of one boot into the heel of another in lieu of a bootjack. Suddenly he stopped and grinned slowly.

'By golly, yo're right, Sad! Palmin' them cards thataway over the saloon, and – he made me think of somebody I'd seen – but – what do yuh make of it?'

'Nothin'. Hawker is a respected citizen of Cinco, and it would be a lifetime job to hang the deadwood on him for that deal, after all this time. Anyway, that Terryville town is deserted now. If he's livin' square, it's all right. A man has a right to the benefit of the doubt, I reckon. But any man who will murder a paymaster – would rob a train.'

'Oh, shore. He's probably covered his back trail pretty deep, but ain't it queer to run on to him like this?'

112

'It's a small world, Swede – and few of us ever get out of it alive.'

'Yeah, that's true.'

'Has Melancholy expressed any opinions?'

'Plenty,' laughed Swede. 'I had quite a talk with him today, and he told me about a few things. The JHC think the J Bar 44 are stealin' their cattle. They don't come right out and say it, of course; but they hint it. It seems that Old Pima Simpson wrote and told Cleland about it, but the old man wouldn't take much notice of it. Melancholy says there's nothin' in it. He says, even if the Gavin outfit did steal JHC cattle, they couldn't dispose of 'em. He says the two outfits hate each other so much that he don't believe either side. He says the J Bar 44 are a salty tribe, but they ain't got anythin' on the JHC.'

'I reckon we'll have to get better acquainted with both sides,' smiled Sad.

'That's right,' grinned Swede, tugging at a boot. 'And in the meantime the fair princess sets in the castle while the brave knight goes huntin' dragons.'

'Yeah, sure,' grinned Sad, 'and he's liable to wish for some tin shirts and cast-iron overalls, before he gets through dragon-huntin'.'

CHAPTER VII

Chuck Gavin and his father came to Cinco City the following day. Chuck was not the modest-looking young man who had sat across the car aisle from Clare. He wore an expensive Stetson, with a tall crown and a seven-inch brim, a white-and-gold neckerchief, corn-colored silk shirt, and his black chaps were the widest in the Cinco range, glittering with silver conchas. His hand-made boots were a little higher in the heel than was customary, and his silver spurs were worth a month's wages for any cowboy. Even his cartridge-belt was hand-stamped, as was his holster, and the belt-buckle was a piece of silver-and-gold creation, which sparkled in the sunlight. When it came to clothes, Chuck 'laid her on plenty,' as the cowboys expressed it.

There was nothing showy about old Bat Gavin. They tied their horses at the Cinco Saloon hitch-rack, and went across to the bank. Frank Welden met them with his customary thin-lipped smile. It was not often that Bat Gavin came to the bank, and Welden wondered how much money he wanted to borrow.

114

'They tell me old Cleland willed his ranch to a girl,' said Gavin.

Welden nodded quickly.

'Seen her?'

'Yes.'

'Uh-huh. Goin' to try and run the place, is she?'

Welden smiled a little.

'Well, what's so dam' funny about it?' demanded Bat.

'Nothing funny, Gavin. Why are you so interested?'

'I want to buy out the JHC – want that water. My springs are runnin' low. I've heard you hold a mortgage ag'in the ranch. How much is it? I want to be able to talk with her.'

Welden, like a turtle, went back into his shell.

'That is a matter between the bank and the JHC Ranch, Gavin. And I think you've got the wrong idea. I've read that will, and it states that this girl is not to sell this ranch to anybody.'

Gavin masticated for a moment, his eyes half-closed.

'Damned old sneak! Knew I wanted it. Where's the girl?'

'Living at the hotel.'

'C'mon, Chuck.'

They went down to the hotel and old Bat

stamped into the lobby. Clare was coming downstairs and Chuck stared at her. Slowly he removed his sombrero, as he walked to the foot of the stairs.

'Yo're Miss Nolan?' he asked, and Clare nodded.

'Gosh, I never suspected. Dad, c'mere. Miss Nolan, this is my dad.'

Bat Gavin looked sharply at Chuck, but shook hands with Clare.

'Kinda seems that you two have met before,' he said dryly.

'We came on the same car in that wreck,' said Chuck. 'I – say, you don't even know my name.'

'You are Mr. Gavin.'

'No, I ain't,' smiled Chuck. 'This is *Mr.* Gavin. I'm Chuck.'

He drew some chairs away from the wall, and they sat down together. Bat Gavin did not beat about the bush, but came to business at once.

'Miss Nolan, I want to buy the JHC Ranch. How much do you want for it, includin' the mortgage?'

'I'm sorry,' she replied softly, 'but it appears that I may not get the JHC Ranch. You see, the body of John Cleland has never arrived here, and they tell me I have no proof that Cleland is dead – not the John

116

Cleland of Cinco City. They even tell me
that the signature on the will is not Cleland's
signature. And even if I did inherit it, the will
states that I cannot sell.'

Old Bat Gavin leaned back in his chair and
stared at the ceiling.

'You didn't get hurt any in that wreck?'
asked Chuck softly.

'Not a bit,' smiled Clare. 'We were all
lucky.'

'Y'betcha. I got hit on the head, but it
wasn't bad. It kinda knocked me hazy, and
I shore was glad to see you over at the depot.
You didn't come here on the train with me.'

'I took a train next forenoon.'

'That's how I missed you.'

'Well,' said Bat Gavin, 'I reckon there's
nothin' to be done.'

He put on his hat and went out, leaving
Chuck with Clare.

'You wasn't related to John Cleland, was
yuh?' asked Chuck.

Clare shook her head. 'No, we were not
related.'

'You knew how he felt towards us, didn't
yuh?'

'I've heard about it since he was killed. It
was mutual, was it not?'

Chuck smiled grimly. 'I suppose it was.'

'And if I had been a relative –'

'No Gavin has ever fought women,' stiffly.

'I didn't mean that. You can hate without fighting.'

Chuck looked at her thoughtfully. 'I'd – I reckon I'd have a hard job hatin' yuh, Miss Nolan.'

'I wouldn't want anybody to hate me. It is such a foolish thing – to hate.'

'Yeah, that's true.'

Chuck got to his feet and held out his hand to her.

'I reckon I better be goin',' he said. 'I hope to see yuh again.'

'I shall be here until this is settled one way or the other.'

'I don't wish yuh any bad luck,' he said slowly, 'but I hope it ain't settled for a long time.'

Clare's eyes followed him as he left the doorway and went across the street.

The conjecture that Cleland's body had been stolen had spread over Cinco City, and was the main topic of conversation, although few believed it. The railroad and express companies kept the wires hot, but found no trace of the shipment. The express messenger was unconscious in a hospital, unable to tell them anything. The body of John H. Cleland had apparently disappeared from the face of the earth.

118

Old Pima Simpson was in from the JHC, anxious to learn more about the missing body, and had acquired plenty of liquor. The old man was fond of Cleland, as he had been with him for years, and he wanted to see that his old friend was properly planted. Ordinarily a peaceful sort of a person, old Pima had listened to the talk of somebody stealing the old man's body until he had grown savage in his cups.

Sontag was sitting on the edge of a table, listening to the conversation, while Melancholy and Swede battled out a game of pool farther down the big room. Beside Sad on the table was a cigar box half-full of poker chips, and Sad was idly clicking them through his fingers, when Bat Gavin came in. Pima looked him over rather belligerently, but said nothing. The conversation continued, and in a few minutes Chuck Gavin came in.

Old Pima shifted his holster and leaned against the bar. Sontag saw the action and watched the old man closely.

'The whole deal is kinda queer,' said Tony Dunham, one of the Circle Dot cowboys. 'Plenty talk about the body bein' stolen, but nobody seems to know who killed the old man down in Los Angeles.'

'Now yo're talkin',' grated Old Pima. 'That's what I want to know, m'self. He never had no enemies down there.'

Old Pima's eyes shifted to Bat Gavin and Chuck.

'We don't have to look very dam' fur to find out who killed him,' continued Pima. 'We know dam' well who'd have killed him if he'd stayed here, and when one of them fellers goes down to Los Angeles –'

'Drop that, Pima!' snapped Melancholy, who left the pool game.

'Drop, hell! Old Cleland was my best friend, and I'll shore back up my war talk right now!'

Old Pima's right hand flashed to his holster, and the big gun came out. The old man was as swift as a striking rattler, but, as his hand grasped the butt of his holstered gun, Sontag flung the box of chips straight at his head. The box traveled a bare ten feet, and the open side landed full in Pima's face, showering him with red, white, and blue chips. The shock staggered him, and before the chips stopped clattering to the floor, Sad was across the narrow space and had wrested the gun from Pima's hand.

The old man staggered back against the bar, cursing bitterly, while Sad stepped back and handed the gun to the bartender. The room was silent for several moments, and then Chuck Gavin spoke.

120

'Thank you, stranger.'

'Yo're welcome,' replied Sad softly.

Old Bat Gavin eyed the crowd. Pima's accusation had been plain enough, and probably voiced the opinion of many men in the saloon. Chuck Gavin's jaw was tightly set and his two thumbs were hooked over the top of his fancy cartridge-belt, as he looked from man to man.

'I reckon we'll be goin',' said Bat Gavin softly.

'Good idea, Dad,' agreed Chuck.

They walked out together and went to the hitch-rack.

'I tell yuh I'm right,' complained Pima. 'If that there damned stilt-legged jigger had kept his nose out of this —'

'You'd be a first-class corpse,' finished Melancholy. 'Chuck Gavin can give yuh a full second start and still beat yuh.'

'I'd like to see him. You fellers know as well as I do that Chuck went to Los Angeles. He was there when the old man was murdered. Who else would kill him? The Gavins got him, that's cinch.'

'You think the Gavins stole the body?' asked Dunham.

'Shore. They want the JHC Ranch. The bank would git it on that mortgage, and Gavin would buy it from the bank.'

'Yuh talk too dam' much,' said Melancholy. 'Yuh can't prove anythin'.'

'Don't have to prove it.'

'Better go home and sleep off that liquor before yore tongue gits yuh into serious trouble.'

'Gimme back my gun, and I'll handle my own trouble.'

Melancholy shook his head at the bartender and went back to his pool game. Pima looked owlishly at Sad Sontag.

'What in hell did you horn in for? Are you a friend of Gavin's?'

'I don't reckon I am,' smiled Sad. 'I jist didn't want to see yuh try to take the law into yore own hands, thasall. Everybody's entitled to their own opinions, but that don't give 'em the right to execute their own ideas of punishment. You was aimin' to take a man's life.'

'He ought to be killed,' Pima retorted stubbornly.

'If a man's opinion gave him the right to execute an enemy, there'd be mighty few of us left.'

Old Pima thought this over deeply.

'By golly, I b'lieve yo're right, at that. Mebbe I was too quick – uh-huh. I wonder if I swallered any of them poker chips. There shore was a shower of 'em for a minute. Ha,

122

ha, ha, ha! Well, I b'lieve I'll go home, if I can have my gun.'

Sad nodded to the bartender, and Pima got his gun. He shoved it deep in his holster and went weaving out of the place. The trouble had been averted, but Sad realized fully that Pima's talk had caused many of the men to think a little deeper in the matter. It was a serious thing to accuse a man of murder, even if the murder had occurred many miles away. The sheriff heard about it, but had little to say, because it was merely a suspicion, with no proof at all. Harry Gilson, the prosecuting attorney, refused to make any move, without more definite proof than the accusations of a drunken old man who hated the Gavin outfit.

Clare heard it talked about in the hotel dining-room that evening, and she asked Sad about it. He told her what had happened in the Cinco Saloon, but made no comment when she told him about the conversation she had had with Chuck Gavin and his father. Clare still had hopes that the body would be found. She had suggested to Tolman that a picture of Cleland be sent to the landlady and the police of Los Angeles, but he told her that as far as he knew, the only existing picture of him was that crayon enlargement.

'No one could possibly identify him by that,' she told Sad. 'It seems as though everything is against me; so I suppose I had better go back to Los Angeles and find another position.'

'I wouldn't do that,' he told her. 'Yuh can always find a job, but yuh can't always find a good battle.'

'Do you like to fight?'

'Not actual fightin', Miss Nolan. I like to outguess the other feller. When I was a little kid, my old dad gave me a puzzle. It was three links of a chain, each link with an open end, kinda curly-cued. He told me to take it apart. Well, I worked on that day after day, and they had to take it away from me at night. Mebbe I worked on it for a month or more, twistin' it this way and that way, but I couldn't work it out. One day I was settin' in the shade of the stable, kinda jinglin' it in my hands, and all to once the danged thing came apart.

'I ain't never forgotten that puzzle. When I get hold of a problem I can't work out nowadays, I kinda set around and jingle it in my mind, and sometimes' – he smiled softly at Clare – 'the darn' thing just falls apart.'

'Then you really think I should stay here and see how it comes out?'

'I shore do. It's a fightin' chance.'

'I think I will. You see, I was rather blue over it all, but after talking with you I feel

124

better over it. Mr. Tolman doesn't want to discourage me, but he says it looks rather hopeless.'

She shook hands with Sad, and went up to her room. The town was quiet that evening. Swede, Melancholy, Ward Bellew, and Andy Tolliver were playing pool. Sad went down to have a talk with the sheriff. Panamint was there, dozing at his desk, and welcomed Sad, who sat down with him. They talked for an hour or more, after which Sad borrowed an old magazine and went back to the hotel, where he sprawled on the bed and read by the light of the smoky old lamp.

His door was open, and in a little while he heard Swede talking with the proprietor downstairs. He thought he heard footsteps in the hallway, but no one went past his door. There was another entrance at the rear, where a rickety stairway led down to the back yard.

Sad tossed his magazine aside and began to roll a cigarette, when from down the hall came a muffled sound, as though something had dropped heavily, and the scream of a woman rang down the hallway. Sad jerked upright and landed on his feet. His belt and gun were on the little table near him, and now he grabbed the gun, twisting it from the holster, as he ran toward the doorway.

125

There was no light in the hallway, except from his own doorway, but the rear entrance was wide open, and in the moonlight, which came through, he saw two men running down the hall. They were near the doorway when he yelled at them to stop. They hesitated, it seems, but did not stop. He was back-lighted by the lamp in his own room, while they were in the dark, and his yell was still ringing down the hallway when a spurt of flame came from near the exit, and a bullet smashed into the plaster near his left elbow, showering him with plaster dust. The men were outside now, crowding each other on the narrow platform, and Sad fired twice in quick succession. The concussion of the heavy cartridges shook the walls, and the smoke blew back toward the main stairway, where Swede was coming at a crouching run, gun in hand.

'What in hell's goin' on?' panted Swede.

Behind him came the hotel man, traveling cautiously.

Sad explained what had happened, and they went down the hall.

'Which is Miss Nolan's room?' asked Sad.

'Fourteen. Next one on the left.'

The door was wide open, emitting an odor of kerosene. Sad lighted a match and looked around. Clare Nolan was on the floor, one shoulder resting against a table leg, her eyes wide with fright. Her right temple was bruised, and she seemed dazed, bewildered. The lamp had been upset, and the cheap carpet was soaked with the spilled kerosene.

They helped Clare to her feet and led her out in the hall, where Sad suggested taking her to his room. They sponged her face with a wet towel, and she tried to smile at them, but was still bewildered.

'Feelin' better?' asked Sad.

Clare nodded quickly. 'Where did they go?' she whispered. 'Those two men. They had masks on, and I – I didn't see them until they were in my room. The door wasn't shut. One of them pointed a gun at me, while the other opened my valise. They threw everything out on the floor, and when they found my pocket-book, I – I guess I tried to scream, and one of them struck me.'

'What did they look like?' asked the hotel man.

'Oh, I do not know. They didn't talk – neither of them spoke a word. I – I thought I must be dreaming, but' – she felt her temple – 'I guess it wasn't any dream.'

More men were coming up the stairway, searching for the cause of the shots. Melancholy was in the lead, as they tramped to Sad's room. There was plenty of powder-smoke in the hallway and in the room. Sad explained to them, and they examined the bullet-scarred plaster beside the door.

'But what was they doin' in yore room, Miss?' asked Melancholy.

'I haven't any idea – and they never said a word.'

'Any money in yore pocket-book?'

'Not more than ten dollars.'

Melancholy turned to Sad.

'You shot twice at 'em, eh?'

'Shore. I heard Miss Nolan scream and ran to the doorway. They was near that outside door, when I yelled at 'em to stop. They took a shot at me, and I shot twice, as they ducked outside. I saw both of 'em, but I couldn't say whether they were big men or small men, 'cause the light was pretty bad, and it was all done so quickly.'

They went down the hall and out on the rickety stairway. The moonlight was bright enough for them to see a dark figure on the ground about twenty feet from the bottom of the stairs. It was a man, lying face down, arms outspread. He groaned as they turned him over.

'Lobo Wolf!' exclaimed Melancholy. 'A Tomahawk Injun.'

'Here's the pocket-book,' grunted Swede, finding it a few feet away.

They picked the breed up and carried him around to the front of the hotel, where he blinked at the lights. The heavy bullet had creased the back of his neck, shocking him badly, but he was far from being a casualty.

Someone brought the doctor, and by that time the sheriff was there, but Lobo was deaf to all questions. Clare examined her pocket-book and found that the contents were intact. As soon as the doctor had bandaged Lobo's neck, the sheriff took him to jail. He was able to walk, but refused to speak.

'Do yuh reckon he's lost his voice?' asked the sheriff.

'I guess he could talk if he wanted to,' smiled the doctor.

Lobo was short, skinny, and his features were typically Indian. His eyes shifted dumbly around, as though appealing for a chance to keep out of jail, but shuffled along ahead of the sheriff down to the jail. Sad went along with them, and, as soon as Lobo was in a cell, Sad tried to question him.

'Lobo,' he said kindly, 'yore best bet is to talk right now. Bimeby you go to penitentiary for mebbe ten years. You tell who sent you to rob lady, and we'll make it easy for you with the law. Know what I mean?'

'Um-m-m-m-m,' grunted Lobo.

'Tell who sent you to rob the lady, and

mebbe you get out of jail pretty soon. You not tell, you stay many years in jail. You *sabe,* Lobo Wolf?'

'You go to hell,' said Lobo.

'Who was with yuh?' asked the sheriff.

'You go to hell, too.'

'Makes it unanimous,' grinned Sad.

Sad went back to the hotel, where the proprietor was fixing up another room for Clare because of the spilled kerosene. She had recovered from her fright, but was still a little nervous. Sad explained that they were unable to get any information from Lobo.

'They didn't have time to open the pocket-book,' said Clare. 'They emptied my valise, but took nothing.'

'The breed had the pocket-book, and when the bullet shocked him, he likely fell all the way downstairs and lost it. His pardner was likely too scared to come back and look for it. But I'm shore glad that yore will is locked up in the sheriff's safe.'

'Do you suppose they were after that will?'

'Looks thataway. Yuh see, Miss Nolan, men in this country ain't in the habit of sneaking in hotel rooms to steal pocket-books. Somebody hired the Injun to do that job – but he won't tell who it was.'

'Then I'm glad it is in a safe place. But if it isn't any good –'

'Somebody is shore scared of it,' laughed Sad.

Someone carried the news to Tom Hawker, and he came in early the next morning. He told the sheriff that Lobo came alone to town, and that he didn't understand why the Injun would be trying to rob a woman. They went in and tried to talk with Lobo, whose head was very sore, but all he said was something to the effect that he didn't feel so very good.

'I dunno much about this particular Injun,' said the sheriff, 'but I'm offerin' odds that he'll talk plenty rather than to go up for a few years. Any cow jury in this State would soak him plenty for hittin' a woman, and add on a few years for stealin' her pocket-book.'

'What good will talkin' do him?' asked Hawker.

'It's like this, Tom; Sad Sontag says somebody stole the body of old John Cleland to stop that girl from gettin' the JHC. She's got a will, which she says was wrote by Cleland – and that's what them two fellers was after last night. Lobo Wolf was workin' for somebody else; *sabe*? And we'd all kinda like to know the name of that man.'

'Oh, I see. Did they get the will?'

'Nope – she didn't have it in the room.'

'Shore a queer deal,' agreed Hawker thoughtfully. 'This Sad Sontag person is that

131

tall stranger, eh?'

'Yeah.'

'What's he got to do with it?'

'Curiosity, I reckon. But he's no fool, Tom. Claims to be an old friend of Buck Hogan, down at Sweetwater.'

'Thasso? Buck's gone East with a load of stock.'

'Uh-huh, that's what Sontag said. He was with Buck in Tejunga, and intended to work for Buck at Sweetwater, but didn't go down there.'

CHAPTER VIII

It was about that same time of day, out at the JHC Ranch, that Elastic Jones was having one of his interminable arguments with Pima Simpson. Pima's libations had left him with a bad head; so he didn't ride with the rest of the crew that morning.

He sat in the living-room of the ranch-house, sock-clad feet on the table; and tried to tell Elastic Jones more about his attack on Chuck Gavin, while Elastic wielded an ineffective broom.

'Yeah, I heard yuh before,' grunted Elastic.

132

'To hear yuh talk, you'd think yuh was Jassacks defyin' the lightnin'. Yo're way past yore prime when it comes to pullin' a gun, Pima. Never did have much sense, and yo're growin' more feeble in the head every day.'

'I'd 'a' got him, jist the same – except for that box of chips. I had three of 'em in the bottom of my drawer laigs when I undressed last night.'

'What's bein' done toward findin' the old man's body?' demanded Elastic, resting on the broom handle.

'Not a dam' thing. The sheriff is as supine as a mountain rattler in Jan'ary. That there female is still at the hotel. I heard that them railroad detectives had a talk with Panamint, and then pulled out. Ain't been no reward offered as far as I can learn. Lotsa folks don't think it was Million Dollar at all, but I b'lieve it was. Chuck Gavin went down there and bushed him, jist as sure as yo're alive – but nobody can prove it.'

'That's why you better keep still.'

'But why would anybody steal the body, for gosh sake?'

'You jist been tellin' me what yuh heard.'

'About somebody ruinin' the evidence? Yeah, that might be it. They call it corpse – corpus – corpus –'

'Corpus Christi?'

133

'Na-a-a-aw! Corpus de – somethin'. Oh, yeah, *corpus delectable.* I heard Tolman, the lawyer, tellin' somebody in the saloon about it. Tolman said the girl had a sort of a will, but it wasn't signed by Cleland. It's shore got me fightin' my head, 'cause – aw, I dunno.'

'Why worry about it?' asked a voice at the rear door, and they turned to see Sad Sontag.

Pima instinctively flinched, but got to his feet. Swede was with Sad, and they came in.

'Elastic, this is the feller who hit me with the box of chips,' said Pima.

'Glad to meetcha, I'm shore,' said Elastic, shaking hands with both of them. 'I'm sorry yuh didn't have a anvil. My name's Hennery Jones, knowed as Elastic. Set down and rest yore heels. I've been tryin' to swamp out this place, but that old booze-fightin' wart-hawg is –'

'Don't show off, Hennery,' advised Pima. 'Jist stop and remember that Sontag ain't got no poker chips in his hand.'

'Oh, is that so-o-o? If yuh ever pull a gun on me, yuh'd better pray for the digestion of a ostrich, 'cause I'll shore make yuh eat that gun.'

Sad and Swede sat down with them and the conversation naturally drifted around to the missing corpse. Both of the old men had been very fond of Cleland, and were anxious to see the body recovered.

'Is that a good picture of him?' asked Swede, pointing at the crayon enlargement on the wall.

'Well,' replied Elastic, 'if you happen to find a corpse that looks like that picture – it ain't Cleland. That's supposed to be him. The old man had some queer ideas of humor, and he *paid* for that thing. One eye lookin' straight at yuh and the other one cross-firin'. It does look like his hair. I reckon the same artist mounted that elk head. The old man said it reminded him of a school teacher he used to have.'

'He shore was a great feller,' sighed Pima. 'Mighty good to me and Elastic.'

'He got value received out of me,' growled Elastic.

'Yea-a-ah! Like hell! You was marked "paid" after the first payday.'

'What do you boys think of that woman's claim?' asked Sad.

'Looks to me like she ought to git it,' said Pima. 'If they stole the body to prevent her from provin' anythin', it shore looks to me like she was in the right.'

'Two masked men tried to rob her of the will last night. Came in her room, held a gun on her, searched her stuff, and stole her pocket-book. She let out a yell, and they knocked her down. Took a shot at me down the hall, but I creased one of 'em plenty, and he's in jail with a sore head.'

'For gosh sake, who was he?' exploded Pima.

'Lobo Wolf.'

'Oh, that dam' half-breed! Why didn't yuh kill him?'

'What would Lobo Wolf want of that will?' asked Elastic wonderingly.

'He didn't say,' smiled Swede. 'In fact, he won't say anythin'.'

'Won't talk, eh? Let me and Pima have him for fifteen minutes, and he'll shore talk.'

'Wouldn't he, though,' grinned Pima.

'What's the opinion of the rest of yore outfit regardin' that girl.'

'Don't say much. Ted Bell didn't want her out here until it was settled. As far as that goes, it ain't no place for a woman – not now it ain't. Larry Delago kinda wanted her. He's a lady-killer. Larry is – in a pig's valise. He thinks the more colors he wears, the more they fall for him. The woman that gits him will shore draw a prize package.'

'Melancholy was tellin' me that some of yuh think the JHC is losin' stock once in a while.'

'That,' said Pima, 'is my unsupported theory.'

'I'm supportin' yuh, feller,' said Elastic emphatically.

'I still stick to my original statement. I've been here a long time, and I know cows. I know how many the old man used to ship, 'cause I helped ship 'em. But I'll tell yuh right now, we ain't shipped for a month of Sundays, and we ain't increasin'. Somethin' is happenin', I tell yuh. But nobody believes me.'

'How could anybody get away with cows on this range?' asked Sad.

'When yuh pin me down to a answer – I don't know. I wish the old man had stayed here. Couldn't 'a' been any worse off. Them Gavins got him, anyway. They was bound to git him sooner or later.'

'Here comes Ted and the boys now,' said Elastic, looking out into the patio.

Bell and Delago came in, and Pima introduced them awkwardly.

'We wondered who was here,' smiled Bell. 'Didn't recognize the horses. We came back through town and heard what happened last night. Yuh had quite a time, eh?' He tossed his hat on the table and sat down.

'Plenty excitin' for the lady,' laughed Sad.

'I'll bet. What do yuh make of it?'

'It seems to be the general opinion that they were tryin' to get their hands on that JHC will she's got.'

'What in hell would an Injun do with that will?' asked Delago.

'For somebody else.'

'Oh-ho-o-o-o-o! They say he won't talk to anybody.'

'Not now. Later he'll talk plenty, when he sees the penitentiary starin' him in the face. He's got jist enough white blood to make him talk. If he was all Injun, I'd say it was no use.'

'That's right,' nodded Bell. 'What's yore opinion on the missin' corpse?'

'You mean – who stole it?'

'Well – yeah.'

Sad laughed softly. 'That's a hard guess for a stranger when the natives haven't any idea. What's yore opinion?'

'I'm one of the natives, yuh know.'

'That's true. What do yuh think of that will? Her lawyer tells me that Cleland's signature is not on that will – that somebody else signed it.'

'I heard that, too, but I don't know a thing about it. Anyway, the old man had this place heavily mortgaged before he left here, with the Cinco City Bank. Three years, I reckon; and from what Frank Welden tells me, the old man never paid any interest. He showed me

138

copies of the letters he sent to Cleland durin'
the last two years, but never got an answer.
He didn't want to foreclose.'

'How big is that mortgage?'

'Welden never told me the exact amount,
but he did say he let the old man have too
much money on the place.'

'Wouldn't be worth much to the girl, even
if she did get it, eh?'

'Unless she can pay off the mortgage and
interest. I expect the bank to foreclose pretty
quick.'

'What other property did the old man own?'

'None around here.'

'Lookin' at it from a cold-blooded angle,
Bell, who would profit most if the legality of
that will was never proved?'

'You mean – if the girl never got the ranch?
I don't know. Gavin wants the ranch, on
account of the water. He's got the money and
he'll pay well for it. If it came to a showdown,
where the court would have to settle the estate
in order to satisfy everybody, the J Bar 44
would probably pay more for it than anybody
else. But I'm not sayin' this to you for any
reason, except to answer yore question.'

'Did you ever know Harold Welden,
Frank's brother.'

'He's never been out here.'

'What kind of a person is Tom Hawker?'

'Tom is all right.'

'The Circle Dot is well liked, I understand.'

'You bet! Uncle Billy Haskell is salt of the earth.'

Mose Heilman came in and was introduced, after which he saw down on his heels against the wall and picked his teeth with a straw.

'This old place is shore homelike,' remarked Sad.

'It ain't bad,' agreed Bell. 'The old man built this part of it. The original ranch-house fell down; so the old man used some of his own ideas in rebuilding. Yuh notice he built it on a stone foundation, leavin' holes for the air to circulate. Makes it cool on the hottest day.'

The talk drifted to range gossip, the scarcity of water and the price of beef, which are always topics of conversation in the range country. All the JHC outfit were pleasant, and Ted Bell urged Sad and Swede to come out again soon. Pima Simpson went out with them to their horse, which they watered before starting back. Sad looked at the foundation of the house and remarked that Cleland must have hauled the stone a long way.

'Not much,' grinned Pima. 'The hole it came from is under the house. It shore was a good idea, in more ways than one.'

Sad and Swede discussed the JHC outfit all the way back to Cinco City.

140

'Everythin' points to the Gavins,' said Sad, 'but to put the deadwood on 'em is another thing entirely. The old man is a tough *hombre*, and the kid's got plenty nerve enough for two men. Panamint pointed out the rest of the outfit to me, and they're pretty forked. If Gleason and McKenna ain't gunmen, I've never seen any. Ellers, the young nephew, is a smoke-eater, from his looks, and McCoy looks dumb enough to shoot when they tell him to shoot.'

'What about Hawker?' asked Swede.

'We know what Hawker was, but for the life of me I can't see where he'd fit in on this deal. The JHC hasn't anythin' to do with him. I'd shore suspect Hawker plenty quick, if he fitted in, which he don't. The Circle Dot is out of the question. I've met Bill Haskell, and he's as square as a dollar. They call his wife Aunt Minnie, and she tries to get the boys to go to church with her and Uncle Billy, but they hide out every Sunday evenin'. No, the whole thing narrows down to the Gavin outfit – and the man who monkeys with that outfit had better wear armor.'

'I think the best thing to do is to drop the whole works,' said Swede.

Sad grinned at Swede, who grunted disgustedly.

'Go ahead. Some day a stick of dynamite
141

will bust under yuh, and you'll be a crippled angel.'

'Not me,' laughed Sad. 'I'll be one of their very best flyers.'

'You'd shore look great – like a sandhill crane. Dang it, I hope that half-breed, two kinds of Injun, decides to talk.'

'He'll talk, but it may take a little time to scare him good.'

They stabled their horses and went over to the sheriff's office, where they found Melancholy stretched out on a cot. He told them that the prosecuting attorney and the sheriff had been in to see Lobo Wolf, but failed to make him talk.

'The lawyer shore told that Injun what he had comin' if he didn't talk, and he shore scared the tripe out of him. Lobo turned green.'

'What did Lobo tell him?' asked Sad.

'Told him to go to hell. Where yuh been?'

'Out to the JHC.'

'I jist wondered. Couldn't find anybody to play pool with t'day. Panamint's over in the courthouse. I reckon they'll hold a hearin' for Lobo tomorrow, an' the prosecutor is goin' to charge him with everythin', except leprosy and spinal menen-gee-tus. Burglary, highway robbery, assault with intent to kill on the person of a lady, assault with a deadly weapon

142

on you. That's enough charges to hold him for a while.

'The lawyer enumerated the whole works to Lobo, and told him he'd give him until nine o'clock tomorrow mornin' to start talkin'. And if he's willin' to tell who hired him and all that, they'll cancel leprosy, and change spinal menen-gee-tus to plain backache. Gawd, what a chance that Injun's got.'

'Was any of the Hawker outfit in to see him?' asked Sad.

'Tom Hawker was there, but Lobo wouldn't talk with him. Tom don't know what it's all about. He says Lobo came to town alone last night. I don't think Tom is goin' to hire any crowd of lawyers to clear Lobo. Anyway, he didn't say he might.'

Swede suggested a game of pool; so Sad went up to the hotel, where he sat down in the shade of the porch and tried to figure out something to work on. The only clue was the fact that the Gavins wanted the JHC. He wondered if they knew that Clare, according to the will, could not sell it. In case she did get the ranch, they could not buy it from her. Their only hope was to prevent her getting it, force the court to settle the estate, and give them a chance to buy the place. Perhaps they were afraid the court might recognize the will, in spite of the missing body, and had hired Lobo Wolf and somebody else to try to steal the will from Clare, at any cost. That sounded reasonable as a theory, unsupported by anything except the thinnest sort of a supposition, and Sad refused to become enthused over it.

Even were they able to find the stolen body and bring it in for evidence, it would merely establish one fact – that Cleland was dead. It would not convict the men who held up that train and imperiled the lives of many people. And with a huge mortgage, interest unpaid for three years, Clare would not be able to handle the JHC. The bank would probably get it, and the bank could sell it to Gavin.

'Heads, they win; tails, she loses,' grunted Sad. 'I'm very much afraid the little lady is up against a deal that'll shore stop her from gettin' much except sunburn out of Arizona.'

After a while he saw the sheriff crossing the street toward his office, so he went down there. Panamint grinned widely as he told Sad how he and the prosecutor had tried to frighten Lobo Wolf into a confession.

'We told him the people would lynch him for hittin' a woman, and he shore got scared. I'll betcha he'll tell us everythin' before his hearin'.'

'It would help a whole lot if he would,' agreed Sad. 'Let me have that envelope out of

144

yore safe, will yuh?'

The sheriff gave it to him and he tucked it inside his shirt. There was no doubt in his mind that the signature on the will was genuine, but to prove it was another matter. Tolman had said it was not the signature of Cleland, but Sad decided to carry the will with him until he was able to find someone who had received a letter from Cleland and had kept it.

As Sad went back up the street, he saw Chuck Gavin dismount in front of a general store. Chuck recognized Sad at a distance, and waved a hand at him before he entered the store. In spite of his bright-hued garments, there was something about the boy that attracted Sad. As he strolled past the store, he glanced through a window and saw Chuck talking with Clare Nolan. He went on to the hotel, where he sat down in one of the chairs which had been placed on the sidewalk, and in a few minutes Clare and Chuck came out. They talked together for a few moments, and came on toward the hotel. Chuck's face was rather grave as he tipped his hat to her at the doorway. She nodded and smiled at Sad as she went in, and Chuck sat down near Sad.

'How are yuh comin'?' asked Sad.

'Oh, I reckon it's all right,' grimly. After a moment he laughed shortly. 'I reckon I'm pretty much of a fool; worryin' because a woman – I'd like to know what difference it makes, whether she believes it or not.'

'Woman are kinda queer,' said Sad thoughtfully.

'I suppose that's true. I've never had much to do with 'em. Dad said to ask yuh out to the ranch any time yuh can come. He don't say much, but I know he appreciated yuh throwin' that box of chips at Simpson.'

'I reckon you could have beaten him on the draw, Gavin.'

'Yeah, I know; and have folks say I killed a drunken old man. I've got enough bad rep' without buildin' it any worse. Miss Nolan was tellin' me what happened last night, and I'm wonderin' if the Injun will talk.'

'Shore, he'll talk.'

'I suppose he will. Well, I've got to go home. Come out, won't yuh?'

'I'll be glad to.'

'Make it any old time, and bring yore pardner.'

Sad watched Chuck ride away, a thoughtful expression in his eyes, wondering if it was merely out of gratitude that Bat Gavin was inviting him out to the J Bar 44 ranch.

It was about nine o'clock that evening when Sad found Clare sitting out in front of the hotel.

'It was so hot in my room,' she explained, 'I simply had to come out.'

'It's shore hot in there, but cool out here.'

Clare was discouraged again and not a little blue. Her talk with Tolman that day had left her with little encouragement to stay longer in Cinco.

'Even if I could prove Mr. Cleland's death and the signature, I couldn't satisfy that mortgage,' she said wearily.

'The ranch may be worth more than the mortgage,' said Sad. 'No bank ever loaned money to the full value. What about his other property?'

'I can't find out a single thing, except the ranch. He had no money in this bank, and I'm sure he had no bank account in Los Angeles.'

'Looks like he left yuh a white elephant.'

'That is what I think.'

'But we ain't through fightin' yet. In fact, we ain't started fightin' yet, 'cause we don't know who to hit. I've an idea that Lobo Wolf will talk, and then we'll have somethin' to work on. The sheriff said yore testimony would hang him, and he's scared enough to tell anythin'.'

'My testimony?'

'That he hit yuh.'

'Well, one of them hit me. I wonder if it

147

would help any for me to talk with him at the jail?'

'I dunno. Say, that's an idea. We'll go down there and you can identify him as the man who hit yuh. We'll fix it up with the sheriff. If Lobo didn't hit yuh, he may deny it – and it might start him off.'

'Let's try it.'

'C'mon; I think Panamint Pelley is down there now.'

They walked down the narrow sidewalk, passing a general store, post-office and feed store. Except in front of the lighted windows, the street was dark. There was a light in the sheriff's window, and the door was partly open. Sad opened the door a little farther and stepped inside with Clare. There was no one in the room, but the door leading to the jail was open.

'Must be out in the jail now,' said Sad softly.

Then, as he took one step forward, something suddenly struck him a terrific blow on the head.

CHAPTER IX

Even with his consciousness wiped out in a fraction of a second, his brain registered the fact that he had been struck by someone behind the door, and it seemed but another second before he awoke to look up at a circle of blurred faces. His mouth tasted salty and there was a strong odor of drugs. Someone was ringing a bell, and he wondered if it would ever stop.

'Comin' out of it,' said a voice. 'He'll have a sore head.'

The faces were plainer now. There were Swede, Melancholy, Andy Tolliver, Panamint Pelley, the doctor, and the hotel proprietor. Sad tried to smile at them, and Swede's face registered relief.

'Feel better?' asked the doctor.

Someone had taken the bell away, and it was growing fainter and fainter.

'Somebody hit me, didn't they?' whispered Sad.

'They shore did,' replied Swede.

Sad felt of his head, and found it intact, with the exception of a swelling on one side. The doctor helped him to a sitting position on the cot and put a pillow behind him.

'They got me cold,' said the sheriff. 'Stuck a gun in my face, took my keys, took Lobo out of the cell, and locked me in, after ropin' my hands and puttin' a gag in my mouth.'

'We found yuh, Sad,' said Melancholy, 'me and Swede. Yuh was there on the floor. Swede went after the doctor and I went huntin' Panamint. They dropped the keys on the floor and I was able to get Panamint out of the cell.'

Sad groaned a little, but got to his feet.

'I didn't see anybody,' he gritted. 'Where is Miss Nolan? Hasn't anybody seen her?'

'Was she with yuh?' asked the sheriff.

Sad nodded.

'I seen yuh go away together,' said the hotel man quickly. 'She ain't come back since then.'

'She wasn't in here,' offered Melancholy. 'Don't that beat hell?'

'Mebbe she got scared and kept on runnin',' suggested Tolliver.

'Aw, they won't hurt her,' said the sheriff. 'Why would they?'

Sad shook his head painfully. He was still dazed and nauseated, and his head throbbed badly.

'You'd better go to bed and take things easy,' suggested the doctor. 'You came near

150

having a fractured skull.'

Sad agreed with him, much against his own will.

'We'll locate the girl,' promised Melancholy. 'She ain't far away, and we'll shore find her.'

'C'mon up to my room, will yuh, sheriff?' asked Sad.

'Shore will,' quickly. 'Feelin' better?'

'I'll be all right in a little while.'

It was just after breakfast at the Gavin ranch, the J Bar 44. 'Casey' Jones stood in the kitchen doorway and watched the riders file away from the corral. Casey Jones was the Chinese cook, a short, moon-faced Celestial, who still wore a queue and swore by all his ancestors. Down at the stable a hen cackled loudly, and a tailless rooster balanced on the top pole of the corral, threw back his head and saluted the sun.

'Bimeby stew,' muttered Casey Jones, eyeing the rooster.

Someone was coming down the stairs, and Casey turned to see Chuck Gavin.

'Rest of the gang gone?' he asked, yawning widely.

'Everybody gone,' nodded Casey. 'W'at yo' like eat, eh?'

'Bacon and eggs, if you've got any good
151

eggs. Them last ones we got in Cinco City must have come all the way from China.'

'China egg velly good. *Mucho fue'te.*' Casey had picked up considerable Spanish, and spoke it in pidgin English.

'They shore were strong,' laughed Chuck, as he filled the washbasin.

'I hea' chicken cluck,' grinned Casey. 'Mebbe egg plenty flesh.'

'One of 'em nestin' in the hayloft,' said Chuck. 'Better take a look.'

Casey Jones hurried down to the stable and disappeared within. Chuck tossed away the water, and went inside to comb his hair. It was not often that he overslept. Casey Jones went along the mangers, looking into each one, but found no eggs; so he came back to the ladder, which consisted of short pieces of boards nailed across the two-by-four studding, and climbed up through the three-foot hole which led to the loft.

He was waist-high inside the loft, when he stopped suddenly. His slant eyes blinked violently. On the hay, not over fifteen feet away, was a lady. She had apparently been trying to get loose from some ropes, but now she stopped and stared at Casey Jones, who squeaked like a trapped rat, and went back down that ladder like a monkey on a rope. He fairly skidded out of the stall, righted himself, and went galloping toward the house, with a shepherd dog barking along behind him. The dog, thinking it was a game, ran between Casey's legs, and the little Chinaman turned a somersault, almost into the kitchen door.

If Casey Jones was frightened, so was Clare Nolan. She had worked for two hours getting loose from those ropes, thinking that she might make her escape, but now she felt that the Chinaman would bring someone to tie her all up again. She had no idea where she was. Things were all confused.

She had seen Sad falling from that blow on the head, a man had held a gun against her, warning her to keep quiet, and had shoved her into the jail corridor, where there were more men.

They had thrown a blanket over her head, tied it tightly, and carried her outside, where she had been put on a horse. A man had ridden behind her, holding her in the saddle. She had no idea how far they had gone. It was stifling hot inside that smelly blanket, and she had nearly smothered.

Finally they had taken her off the horse, and she had stumbled around in the dark, until they had forced her to climb a ladder. There had been no light, but one man had kept warning her not to make a sound. Finally they had bound her with ropes and had gone away without making an explanation, and left her lying on the hay.

Several times she had heard voices, and the sound of someone singing, but it had finally died away, and she had slept a little. Daylight had been filtering through the cracks in the roof when she had awakened. There had been more voices, dim at first, but a little later the men had come down to get their horses, and she had heard them quite plainly, but had been unable to tell who they were.

She had been stiff and sore from the ropes, but she had soon found that they had not tied her very securely, and in a little while she had been able to loosen them. At the other end of the big loft was an opening about five feet square, through which she could see the sunlit hills and the blue sky. She had been almost free of the ropes when Casey Jones had popped up through the hole in the floor, like a moon-faced jack-in-the-box, giving her an awful shock.

Clare threw off the last coil and got to her feet. She was stiff and sore in every joint, but she tiptoed to the opening at the front and peered out. There was a corral off to the left, and straight ahead was a barbed-wire fence. Below her and a little distance away were a lumber wagon and a two-wheeled cart. As she peered around the corner, Chuck Gavin came

154

in sight, hatless, without his chaps, his wet hair shining in the sun. Suddenly he stopped short, looking back. He had been hurrying, but now he seemed to slump within himself, like a runner after the finish of a long, hard race. He came on slowly to the corner of the stable, where he stopped with his back to the wall, while in behind him came four riders.

These were Sad, Panamint Pelley, Swede, and Melancholy. Clare's heart jumped with joy at sight of them. She noticed that Sad Sontag was wearing his hat tilted on the left side of his head, and there was no smile on his face. Chuck merely nodded to them, as they stopped near him.

'Hello, Chuck,' said the sheriff coldly.

'Hello, Panamint. Ridin' early, ain't yuh?'

'This is somethin' that needs early riders.'

'What's wrong?'

'Somebody busted the jail last night and took Lobo Wolf. They hit Sontag over the head, knocked him cold as a wedge, and then they kidnaped Miss Nolan.'

Chuck said nothing, merely looked from man to man. He knew Clare was in that hayloft; knew they'd find her.

'What do yuh know about it?' asked the sheriff.

'Lobo Wolf is nothin' to me,' said Chuck slowly. 'I wouldn't hit Sontag, and God knows

155

I wouldn't kidnap a girl. You – you ain't lookin' for her here, are yuh?'

'We're lookin' for her everywhere, Chuck. Mind if we search the place?'

'I can't stop yuh,' he said slowly. 'I'll help yuh look.'

'You'll stay right here, Chuck. I don't say you done it, and I don't say yuh know where she is, but it'll shore go hard with the man or men who took her when we find 'em. Hangin' is too dam' good for a kidnaper of women.'

'I didn't kidnap any woman,' said Chuck hotly. 'My gosh, why would I steal her? I'm no savage! The only woman on earth I ever wanted to have a good opinion of me, and you think I'd hurt her.'

For several moments there was silence. Clare was leaning back from the opening, her mind working swiftly.

The sheriff was speaking. 'We saw that Chinaman runnin' toward the house, when he seen us. Wasn't he warnin' you?'

Chuck's voice was steady, as he replied, 'He was gettin' some eggs for my breakfast.'

'Uh-huh. Well, anyway, we'll look around. You stay where yuh are, Chuck, and I'll look the place over.'

The sheriff dismounted and came inside the stable. It did not take him long to search the stalls, and then he climbed up the ladder.

156

There was nothing in the loft except a pile of loose hay at the rear. Near the entrance was a length of lariat rope, thrown carelessly aside. The sheriff looked at it, but tossed it aside, and went back down the ladder.

Chuck's jaw sagged a little when the sheriff came out alone. Sontag was watching Chuck when the sheriff came out and he knew Chuck was surprised. He straightened a little and wet his dry lips with his tongue.

'Nothin' in there,' said the sheriff. 'Let's take a look at the house.'

'Go ahead,' said Chuck hoarsely. 'Might as well look it all over while yo're here, and when yuh finish, I'll have Casey cook yuh some breakfast.'

'Had it before we left,' growled the sheriff as they went to the house.

But a search of the house netted them nothing. They even went down in the cellar under the kitchen, while Casey Jones looked blankly at them

'Well, I'm glad she ain't here, even if we do want her mighty bad,' said the sheriff, after the search. 'And yuh don't need to feel bad about it, 'cause we're goin' to treat everybody the same. It's a dam' serious thing.'

'You don't need to tell me that,' said Chuck slowly.

Casey Jones was frying bacon and eggs as

though nothing unusual had happened, and the four riders filed out through the gate, heading back for Cinco City.

Chuck sat down weakly on the back steps and watched them out of sight. Casey Jones came out and stood in the doorway.

'Casey,' said Chuck weakly, 'did you shore see a woman?'

'See plenty good – you dam' bet. Whasamall with she'iff?'

'I don't know, unless he went blind.'

Chuck got to his feet and went back to the stable, where he climbed the loft ladder. Clare had seen him from the opening, and was standing there near the hay when he came up. For a long time they stared at each other. There was hay clinging to Clare's hair and to her dress. Chuck took a deep breath and stood there, his hands in his pockets.

'If you'd move, I'd be sure it's you,' he said foolishly.

Clare brushed some hair out of her eyes and tried to smile.

'And the sheriff couldn't find you,' he said slowly. 'Where were you then?'

'I – I hid under the hay,' gesturing wearily toward the rear. 'I was over by the window and I heard what they said – and what you said.'

Chuck took a deep breath. 'And you hid in

158

the hay to save me?'

'I – I don't know. I guess I didn't want – he said hanging was too good for a kidnaper, and I don't want anybody hung on my account.'

Chuck shook his head slowly, his eyes fixed on her face.

'Miss Nolan, will yuh believe me when I say I didn't know you was here until Casey Jones came and told me?'

'Is Casey Jones a Chinaman?'

'Yeah. You scared him stiff.'

'Well, he scared me stiff, too.'

They looked at each other and laughed foolishly.

'He's cookin' breakfast,' said Chuck.

'I could smell the bacon a long time ago.'

'Let's go and get it.'

Clare climbed down the ladder and Chuck followed her. Casey Jones watched them from the kitchen door, a smile on his bland face, as they came up to him.

'Casey, this is Miss Nolan,' said Chuck.

'Yessa,' bobbed Casey. 'I meet befo'. Yo' like 'em stlaight up or tu'n ova'?'

'What does he mean?' asked Clare.

'Eggs,' grinned Chuck.

'Oh, I don't care – I could almost eat them raw. I know I must be a perfect fright.'

'Absolutely perfect,' agreed Chuck heartily.

'And I've had the most perfect one of my life. I'm years and years older than I was when I got up this mornin'. But I'm glad of it all, because you're here for breakfast. Want to wash? Yeah, we've got plenty combs and a mirror. All the comforts of home. And while we eat breakfast, you can tell me all about it. I remember the sheriff tellin' me somethin' about it, but I was so scared I never heard him. And when he came out of that stable alone – well, my heart skipped seven distinct beats. It ain't normal yet, and if I get to talkin' foolish – you'll overlook it, I hope.'

'I'm a little foolish myself,' smiled Clare, as Chuck filled the basin for her.

While they ate breakfast together, Clare told him what had happened at the sheriff's office. She didn't know how many men there were, but she thought there were three. The one man who hit Sad Sontag was masked, but she wasn't sure about the others. Chuck did not make any comments, except to remark that she was lucky to get out of it so easily.

'The question is this, How am I going to get you back to town without makin' a lot of explanations?' queried Chuck.

'I might fix that up for yuh,' said a voice at the doorway, and they turned quickly to see Sad Sontag, leaning lazily on one elbow.

160

Chuck started to his feet, but Sad motioned him to sit down.

'Set down,' he said easily.

'Where did you come from?' asked Chuck anxiously. 'Where are the others?'

'Gone to town. I told 'em I was goin' over to the JHC, but I doubled back here. Yuh see, I played a hunch that the lady was here.'

'You had that hunch?' asked Chuck wonderingly. 'Just why, Sontag?'

'Well, you was scared to have the sheriff search the stable, and yuh shore showed relief when he came out without her. Yuh see, our sheriff ain't much on readin' faces. Mebbe yuh can be glad he ain't, 'cause he's a serious sort of a jigger.' He turned to Clare. 'Didja hide in the hay?'

'I did,' defiantly.

Sad rubbed his chin thoughtfully.

'Why didja hide?'

'Because.'

'That's a woman's answer. Was it 'cause yuh didn't want Gavin to go to jail for stealin' a woman?'

Clare got to her feet. 'Perhaps,' she said.

'Uh-huh.' Sad grinned and shook his head slowly. 'I reckon it's all right. Now I've got to take yuh back and lie to everybody about findin' yuh.'

'You don't need to lie,' said Chuck quickly.

161

'Tell 'em where yuh found her.'

'Eatin' breakfast with you, eh? Sittin' here and eatin' breakfast of her own free will. They'd believe that. Nope, that won't do, Gavin. I'll tell 'em I found her walkin' along the road, tryin' to find the town. I'll say she was plumb lost, wanderin' around. She can say that the kidnapers dumped her off out in the hills and she got loose from the ropes.'

'Why not tell the truth?' asked Chuck coldly.

'Don't be a fool, Gavin. Yo're in bad enough as it is. Even if Miss Nolan didn't prefer charges against yuh, you'd be liable for breakin' open the jail and lettin' a prisoner out. If they knew she was here, they'd cinch you for that jail break as shore as God made little apples.'

Chuck got up from the table and came over to Sad.

'Sontag, what's yo're business?' he asked.

'Everybody's,' seriously.

'I don't *sabe* that answer.'

'That's the only answer I've got.'

'Everybody's business, eh? Deputized?'

'Yeah.'

'They call it compoundin' a felony, don't they?' asked Chuck grimly.

'Because I don't arrest yuh?'

162

'Yo're a deputy sheriff – and you've got evidence.'

'Court evidence,' drawled Sad. He turned to Clare. 'Do yuh want me to arrest this man, Miss Nolan?'

'If I did, I wouldn't have hid in that hay.'

'Do yuh still think he kidnaped yuh?'

'I – I don't know what to think,' she confessed.

'Is there any reason why I should have kidnaped her?' asked Chuck.

'And that,' smiled Sad, 'is why I'm not arrestin' yuh. You wouldn't hardly sacrifice yore liberty for a chance to eat breakfast with her, and that's what I find yuh doin'. Miss Nolan, if yo're ready, we'll start for Cinco City before anybody sees yuh here. My horse will carry double.'

'I'll furnish her a horse,' offered Chuck.

'Fine. I discover her between here and town ridin' one of yore horses, eh? I'll explain about findin' the lady, but I'll be danged if I'll alibi the horse and saddle. C'mon, Miss Nolan; never mind the skirts.'

He helped her into the saddle and climbed on behind her. Chuck waved at them from the front porch of the ranch-house as they rode away.

163

CHAPTER X

'That was a nervy thing for you to do – hide from the sheriff,' said Sad. 'Now go ahead and tell me what happened after I got hit.'

Clare told him what she knew about it, which wasn't very much. She told of the long ride inside the hot, smelly blanket, and how frightened she was in the dark alone; of the coming of daylight and the sound of voices. Sad laughed over the description of Casey Jones's sudden entrance and exit. She explained that she was at the opening of the loft and heard what was said to Chuck.

'When the sheriff said he'd deserve worse than hanging, I – I ran back and covered up in the hay. What is worse than hanging, Mr. Sontag?'

'Chilblains. I had 'em one winter in eastern Oregon.'

'You are making fun of me.'

'Yeah, and I'm goin' to keep on makin' fun of yuh, as long as yuh call me Mr. Sontag. My name is Sad.'

'Well, you call me Miss Nolan – and my name is Clare.'

'I never knew it, Clare. Love of gosh, look who's here!'

They had ridden around a curve just below the forks of the road, and met Ted Bell, Larry Delago, and Pima Simpson. They were too close to be avoided.

'Well, by the great horn-spoon – thar she is!' yelped Pima.

'Where did you find her?' asked Ted Bell.

Sad drew rein and grinned at the three cowboys.

'Walkin' along the road,' he replied, 'back here about a mile. Them fool kidnapers dumped her off in the hills, but she managed to work the ropes loose and I found her out there huntin' for Cinco City.'

'Imagine that!' exclaimed Delago. 'She got off lucky. Everybody in town is either out huntin' for her or goin' out. We just found it out a while ago, and was goin' to head into the hills.'

'I was rather fortunate,' said Clare wearily.

'You shore was,' admitted Ted Bell. 'Got any idea who it was?'

Clare shook her head.

'Wasn't yuh scared – out in the hills at night?'

'I believe I was.'

'Got plenty grit,' admired Pima. 'Jist a-plenty. I like wimmen with a lot of grit.'

165

Clare smiled at him and he grew embarrassed.

'Well, we've got to be knockin' along,' declared Sad. 'This here little lady is needin' a little sleep and rest.'

'And grub,' added Pima. 'Ma'am, I'll bet yo're hungry enough to eat hay.'

'I – I haven't eaten any yet,' she replied.

'Well, I'm shore glad yo're safe,' said Bell, a statement which was echoed by Delago and Pima. Clare thanked them, and they rode on.

'Why did he mention hay?' asked Clare anxiously.

'Jist an expression,' chuckled Sad, 'but it shore fit in good.'

'I was startled.'

'He didn't mean anythin'. I watched his face.'

'Can you read character?'

'Sometimes.'

'What do you think of Chuck Gavin?'

'Oh, he's a reckless kid. Chase an enemy through a burnin' buildin', or go to hell for a friend. Excuse my expression, Clare. Kinda bitter toward the world, I reckon. Hate to be thanked for doin' a favor. Born and raised to be a Gavin, which means he has to uphold the family reputation for bein' hard-jawed. A lot of Gavins have died with their boots on, and he thinks he'll have to do the same. But I've

166

seen him scared to death. I don't think it was fear of the consequences, but fear that you'd think he was guilty of stealin' yuh. For some danged reason, that reckless kid wants yuh to have a good opinion of him.'

Clare flushed, but did not reply. They were close to town now and the subject was dropped. Sad lifted her down at the hotel, and she went to her room, while Sad was left to explain things to everybody. The sheriff, together with Swede and Melancholy, had gone out to the Tomahawk, and it was two hours later when they came back to town.

The sheriff was happy over the return of Clare, and took the prosecuting attorney to the hotel to talk with her. The county was offering a thousand dollars for information which would lead to the conviction of the men who took Lobo Wolf from the jail and kidnaped Clare; but Clare was unable to assist them in their search.

Two other reward notices had made their appearance. One, sent out by the express company, offered five thousand for the conviction of the men who had smashed their safe and crippled the messenger; and the other was of one thousand dollars, offered by the county, for the conviction of the men who stole J. H. Cleland's body from the express car. The reward was worded 'or casket box, alleged to contain a human body.'

The sheriff told Sad he had talked with Tom Hawker, who was as much at sea as anybody else. He had not seen Lobo Wolf, and was of the opinion that the jail-breakers had helped Lobo escape from the country to prevent him from telling what he knew.

'That don't require a lot of intelligence,' replied Sad. 'They knew the Injun would tell everythin' to get out of this trouble. Too bad we didn't think to guard him closer.'

Sad had never talked with Frank Welden, the banker, but he drifted into the bank and found Welden there alone.

Welden was inclined to be affable and congratulated Sad on finding Miss Nolan. He questioned Sad as to where and how he found the lady, and seemed bitter against anyone who would kidnap a lady.

'Things like that give a place a black eye,' he said. 'I'm surely glad she wasn't injured in any way.'

'She wasn't hurt, but it was quite a bad shock. A few more like that, and she'll go away with a bad impression of this country. First, she gets in a train wreck, which might have been pretty bad, and then she finds she has lost her inheritance. Now she's kidnaped and left all night in the hills. I don't know what she thinks about it, but I reckon she

168

feels like the feller who went into a dance-hall.

'The floor manager led him outside, but he came back again. Next time the floor manager kicked him out and down the steps, but he soon came back. The last time the floor manager hit him on the jaw, busted his nose, and threw him out through a window. Someone asked him if he was going back, and he replied, "Hell, no; I don't think they want me in there." '

The banker chuckled softly. 'I guess that's right; she isn't wanted here – by some people.'

'You knew John Cleland pretty well, didn't yuh?' asked Sad.

'As well as anybody knew him.'

'Tolman told Miss Nolan that it ain't Cleland's signature on the will.'

'That is correct. Have you read the will?'

'Yeah, I've read it. Have you a copy of Cleland's signature?'

'I'll show you a letter from him, and you can easily see that the two signatures are not at all alike.'

He produced a file from which he selected a typewritten letter, signed by John H. Cleland. The letter was merely a note, asking Welden to advise Ted Bell about a shipment of cattle. The date on it was nearly a year previous. Sad could see at a glance that the signatures were not alike in any way. He gave the letter back to Welden, who replaced it in his file.

'Didn't Cleland bank with you?' asked Sad.

'John Cleland was a queer man,' sighed the banker. 'He ran his business on a cash basis. The cattle-buyers knew he wanted cash; so they paid him that way, and he paid all his bills in cash. He would exhibit a silver dollar and announce that as soon as he had a million of them he'd retire. That is where he got his nickname.

'After he left here, rather suddenly, as you have probably heard, he told Ted Bell to open an account with our bank and run the business.'

'Didn't he own more than the JHC?'

'I've often wondered. I have heard that he invested money in bonds, but I doubt it.'

'Some folks think he was wealthy.'

'I know they do – but where is it? He must have taken money to Los Angeles when he left here.'

'In case his body is never recovered, what will be done with the ranch?'

'I think I can answer that question. The Cinco City Bank has a big mortgage on the JHC Ranch, the interest of which has never been paid, and we are going to foreclose right away. I could show you copies of the many letters I have sent to John Cleland, begging him to pay the interest. The bank does not want the JHC, but may have to take it.'

Sad rubbed his sore head, tilting his big hat over one eye.

'In case the bank has to take it over,' he said slowly, 'how would be the chances to buy it? I mean, would the bank be willin' to sell it for the amount of the mortgage, plus interest?'

Frank Welden looked keenly at Sad, apparently at a loss for a moment.

'Why, I don't know,' he replied thoughtfully. 'That is a future matter. Are you looking for a ranch?'

'I might be. I like the looks of the JHC, and if the price was right, I might make a deal with yuh.'

'It is a little too early in the matter to consider a sale.'

'How about givin' me an option to buy. Yuh can word it to cover the deal, in case the bank is stuck with the property.'

Welden shook his head quickly. 'No, I couldn't do that. It might happen that the bank would want to keep it.'

'I see. Well, if I'm around here, and yuh do want to sell it, can I have the first chance at it?'

'Certainly.'

Sad went back to the hotel, grinning to

himself. He didn't have enough money to pay one year's interest on that mortgage, but Sad wanted to feel out the banker. Why would the bank want the JHC, he wondered. Anyway, he had caused Welden to consider him – Sad – a wealthy man.

'He'll probably tip his hat to me now,' grinned Sad to himself.

He found Swede in front of the hotel, tilted back in a chair, hat over his eyes.

'H'lo, brave knight,' grinned Swede. 'I seen yuh goin' over to the bank; so I set down here to cover yore getaway, in case yuh held it up. That's about the only excuse you'd have for goin' in there. Now, would yuh mind tellin' me where yuh found the lady? Yuh know, I didn't swaller that story about yuh findin' her on the road between the J Bar 44 and the forks of the JHC road.'

'Why not?' asked Sad innocently.

' 'Cause yuh started for the JHC, that's why. What in hell would yuh be doin' back on the road we jist came over?'

'My mistake,' grinned Sad, and proceeded to explain to Swede why he went back to the J Bar 44, and what he found.

Swede was interested enough to take off his hat and whistle softly.

'I thought Chuck acted kinda funny,' he said.

'Yuh didn't – until now.'

'No, I s'pose not. And she hid in the hay. By golly, that's good! If Panamint knew that, he'd never hunt for her again.'

'I hope he don't have to, Swede.'

'Same here. What's the answer to the whole thing? Ain't yuh got nothin' to work on? I'd like a crack at them rewards.'

Sad shook his head slowly. 'They've shore covered their tracks. There's just four outfits to suspect; the JHC, J Bar 44, Tomahawk, and the Circle Dot. I've tried to suspect all of 'em, but I don't get anywhere with my suspicions. Tomorrow I'm goin' to start ridin'. I can't think here in town, and I'll be darned if I think the answer is here.'

'Do I ride with yuh?'

'You shore do. And from now on, be suspicious of everybody. The first thing we know, there'll be a puff of smoke – and we're angels. Don't forget that. Now let's go fold ourselves around a meal.'

Mike Joe was what might be termed a hard-looking Indian. He was lean, stringy, thin-faced, with cheek-bones so prominent that his eyes were nearly hidden. His mouth was loose-lipped. He had a pointed chin and a thin, scrawny neck. He wore a strip of handkerchief around his coarse hair, and his

173

shirt had long since passed the day when it needed washing. He wore ragged old overalls and cowboy boots.

Just now he sat in the shade of the stable at the Tomahawk Ranch, huddled up on an old blanket, a bottle of cheap whiskey between his feet. Tom Hawker did not allow his Indians to drink liquor; but Hawker was not at the ranch, and Mike Joe was Indian and did not fear consequences. In fact, Mike Joe was in mourning. He took another swig and put the bottle down, liquor dripping from his lower lip, which sagged badly, his eyes half-closed and sullen.

He did not move or look around when Sad and Swede rode up to him. They dismounted and squatted on their heels near him. Understanding Indians, they rolled cigarettes and smoked silently, until Mike Joe condescended to turn his head and discover them. He started to offer them a drink, thought better of it, and withdrew his skinny hand, clutching the bottle.

'Dam' hot,' he said thickly.

'All of that,' smiled Sad. 'Where's everybody?'

The Indian thought it over.

'Mike Joe here,' he said thickly. 'Hawker be dam'.'

174

Mike Joe evidently considered himself all-sufficient.

'You Lobo Wolf's pardner?' asked Sad.

Mike Joe helped himself to a big drink, wiped his lips with the back of his skinny hand, and hunched himself a little more.

'Lobo gone,' he replied heavily.

'Somebody stole him out of the Cinco City jail.'

'Mm-m-m-m-m. Dam' hot t'day.'

'Mebbe Lobo has gone a long ways from here, eh?'

'Um-m-m-m-m-m.'

'You like Lobo, Mike?'

'Lobo gone 'way' – indicating with a sweeping gesture.

'Lobo was a good man, they tell me.'

'Um-m-m-m-m.'

'You and him was good friends, eh?'

Mike Joe considered this question for a long time. Then he said, 'Hawker gone in hills. Pretty dam' hot. You have drink?'

'Too hot to drink whiskey.'

'Good!' with evident relief. 'Mike Joe not scare' from heat.'

And to prove it, he took three big swallows of the fiery liquor. That was the straw which broke the camel's back, and in a few minutes Mike Joe was dead to the world, snoring lustily. There was no other sign of

175

life about the place, except cows bawling down behind the corral, and a lean mongrel dog, which sniffed at them suspiciously, growled, and then sat down to hunt a flea. The tumbledown old ranch-house was not inviting, and everything about the place had a down-at-the-heel look.

'No use of a white man livin' like this,' said Sad, as they mounted. 'No use tryin' to get anythin' out of a drunken Injun. They're bad enough when they're sober.'

'That war-whoop is worried about somethin',' declared Swede.

'He's worried about Lobo Wolf. Lobo's gone, and Mike probably don't know where he is; so Mike proceeds to get drunk and get sorry for himself. They were bunkies, I understand.'

It was at least a hundred and twenty in the shade – and no shade; so they decided to go back to Cinco City. Sad told Swede about seeing Cleland's signature at the bank, and that it did not tally with the one on the will. Sad wondered if there was a possibility that the man who had killed Cleland had also written the will and left it there for a purpose.

As they rode along the dusty highway toward Cinco City, he took the will from his pocket and studied it closely. But what motive would any man have in killing the

176

old man and faking a will in favor of Clare Nolan, he wondered. As he studied the will in the strong sunlight, he noticed some marks in the paper near the upper left-hand corner.

It was apparently an impression made through another sheet of paper, possibly with the point of a sharp pencil. The marks were meaningless, except for the letters HLW, written together in script, another of HW written together in several different ways. It might have been done by someone toying with a pencil, while talking or listening to a conversation.

There were more impressions near the center of the sheet, but these were not so deep. However, he was able to decipher Clare Nolan's name, and the initials JHC. Below them, as though on another line, was the word 'bonds.' The rest of the page failed to show any impressions.

Swede watched the expressions on Sad's face, but said nothing until he folded the will and replaced it in his pocket.

'Somethin' new?' he queried.

Sad smiled thoughtfully. 'As Mike Joe said – it's pretty dam' hot.'

Sad found Clare on the hotel porch, busy on a piece of embroidery work. She was anxious to hear of any new developments, but he shook his head and sat down with her.

'Do you know anybody with the initials H.L.W.?' he asked. Clare looked up quickly.

'Why, those are Harold Welden's initials.'

'I thought so. He's the Los Angeles attorney and a brother of Welden at the bank, eh? Didn't you say he was a friend of Cleland?'

'I believe they knew each other quite well.'

'You knew Harold Welden, didn't you?'

'Oh, yes – quite well,' she smiled.

Sad considered her gravely.

'How well?'

Clare bent over her work and did not look up as she replied. 'He proposed to me the night John Cleland was murdered.'

'Well!' grunted Sad rather explosively. 'You – you didn't accept him?'

'Hardly.'

Sad leaned back in his chair and clasped his long fingers around one knee.

'Clare, could anybody else have written that will?'

She looked up quickly. 'What do you mean?'

'They say it isn't Cleland's signature, yuh know. Wait a minute. What time in the evenin' did Welden propose?'

'It was just after I left the office – about five-thirty. He walked home with me.'

'And Cleland was killed late at night.'

'Yes, it must have been nearly eleven

o'clock. Several people heard the sound of the shots.'

Sad shook his head wearily. 'I don't no more than get an idea, when somethin' comes along and tears it to pieces. Clare, is there anybody in the world except yourself who would profit by you inheritin' all of old man Cleland's property?'

Clare shook her head quickly. 'Not a person in the world.'

'What kind of a feller is Harold Welden?'

'Rather good-looking, but travels with a fast crowd, drinks and gambles. He was drunk when the officers brought him up to Mr. Cleland's apartment after Mr. Cleland was dead.'

'Why did they take him up there?'

'They wanted to ask him questions about Mr. Cleland. They found that Mr. Welden and I were fairly intimate with Mr. Cleland, and they wanted to know all about it.'

Sad rolled a cigarette, his keen gray eyes half-closed as he scratched a match along the sole of his boot and lighted the paper-covered roll of tobacco.

'Clare, do you remember any questions they asked him?'

'No, I don't remember just what was said. You see, I was so upset myself. I do remember that they asked him if he had ever done any

179

legal work for Mr. Cleland, and he said he hadn't. They also asked him when he had seen Mr. Cleland last, and he said he hadn't seen him for two days.'

'Do you know if those answers were true?'

'I suppose they were. Mr. Cleland had never mentioned Harold doing any legal work for him. Why did you ask me about his initials?'

Sad produced the will and showed her the impressions in the paper.

'Harold wrote them,' she declared. 'I have seen him do it before. It is sort of a monogram.'

'Uh-huh. What about that kinda paper; did you ever see any of it around Cleland's apartment?'

'No, I never have. It is a common brand of typewriter paper. In fact it is so cheap that some of the offices use it for scratch paper – to make notes on. The surface is so full of clay, or something like that, that it does not stand erasing well. That is why it took the impression so plainly.'

'Would a lawyer use it for makin' notes?'

'I suppose so.'

'Uh-huh.'

Clare leaned back in her chair and looked at the tall cowboy, who was staring down at his boots, his lips shut tightly.

'You are not thinking of connecting Harold Welden with anything, are you?' she asked.

'I'm goin' to connect somebody with it pretty quick, or blow up.' He looked up at her, smiling quickly. 'Has anybody asked yuh where the will is bein' kept?'

'No one has mentioned it.'

'If they do – don't tell 'em. Hasn't Tolman asked about it?'

'He asked me if I was going to have it recorded, and I told him I didn't know. He said there wasn't much use of it.'

Sad got to his feet and leaned against a porch post. Chuck Gavin was dismounting at a hitch-rack across the street, and now he came toward them.

'I'll see yuh later, Clare,' said Sad, and started down the sidewalk.

'Yuh don't need to run away,' called Chuck.

'I'll confine myself to a walk,' grinned Sad.

He was nearly down to the sheriff's office when a man rode into town from the north end. He was hatless, swaying in his saddle, but keeping to the middle of the road. The sheriff came to the door of his office, as Sad stepped off the sidewalk and went into the street to intercept the rider, who was looking blindly ahead.

CHAPTER XI

It was Old Pima Simpson, his head and face streaked with blood, his left arm dangling loosely at his side. The sorrel horse was bleeding from a bad cut on the shoulder, and seemed willing to stop. The sheriff arrived almost as soon as Sad.

'For Gawd's sake, he's all shot up!' snorted the sheriff. 'Hang on to the other side of him, Sad. Don'tcha know me, Pima?'

At that moment Pima went as limp as a rag, slumped off into the sheriff's arms and they went down in the dust together, with Pima on top. Chuck Gavin was running down the sidewalk, and men were coming from across the street, as Sad picked Pima up in his arms and carried him over to the office. Everyone asked questions, which no one could answer.

The sheriff sent one of the men for a doctor, while he and Sad washed the blood off Pima's face and head, disclosing a nasty scalp wound. They knew without an examination that the old man's left arm had been broken. But Old Pima was luckily unconscious and stayed that way, while the doctor set and bandaged the arm and sewed up his scalp.

182

A few minutes later, Ted Bell and Larry Delago rode in from the JHC. They saw the crowd at the sheriff's office and came down there. Bell told the sheriff that Pima was at the ranch when they rode away early that morning, and they didn't know he had left the ranch until they came back and Elastic told them Pima had gone to town.

Just what happened to Pima was as much of a mystery to them as to everyone else. They put Pima in a room at the hotel. The doctor believed that Pima would recover in a short time, although he was badly weakened from loss of blood, and the bullet scrape had shocked him badly. The bullet had broken his arm, but as far as the doctor was able to determine, it had not shattered the bone. The horse had been scored on the shoulder, but not crippled.

Sad and the sheriff were sitting with Pima when he recovered. He was still groggy and sick, but mentally all right. The sheriff explained how they found him, but Pima had no recollection of coming to town.

'Some dam' rustler got me,' he whispered. 'Out there at that old corral in Keno Canyon. I saw some men down there and they took a shot at me. They hit my horse and it started buckin'. Then along comes another bullet, which hit me in the arm, I reckon. I piled the spurs into that sorrel, and was goin' strong when all to once there was a big explosion. It blew me so dam' high, I had an idea I'd never git back, and all to once I landed *kerflop* in this bed.'

'Are yuh shore they was rustlers?'

'I ain't shore of nothin' ' – weakly – 'but honest men don't attack yuh thataway. There was cows in that corral, but I never did git close enough to see what was what. But I'll pay 'em back, y'betcha. Oncet I git back on m'two laigs, I'll pay 'em back a-plenty.'

'You take things easy,' advised Sad.

'Yeah, I guess so. That doctor shore took one awful tuck in my scalp. I can't even open m'mouth good, and m'ears feel all pricked up.'

'He shore did take wrinkles out of yore face,' grinned Sad.

The sheriff sent Melancholy to stay with Pima, while he and Sad and Swede rode out to Keno Canyon. The trail led off the main road about halfway between the Tomahawk road and the road to the J Bar 44. It led up through a wide dry wash to the mouth of a small canyon, whcrc they traveled along the left side for a mile, finally coming out of the brush about a hundred yards above the old corral. The corral itself was about sixty feet square, but was in fairly serviceable condition.

184

There were plenty of evidences that cattle had been there recently, and there were tracks of shod horses around the fence, where the ground was softer. Sad found a freshly fired thirty-thirty rifle cartridge, but was unable to find any more. They searched carefully for signs of a branding-fire, but found none. A further search up the canyon disclosed a number of JHC cattle, feeding peacefully.

'Got me skunked,' admitted the sheriff. 'I shore hate to dispute an old-timer like Pima, but –'

'No dispute comin',' said Sad. 'Somebody shot the old boy. He says he was shot by men at this corral. All right – why? They've had cattle in here – why? It's not brandin'-time. Yuh can't shut yore eyes to the fact that somebody shot Old Pima Simpson, 'cause they didn't want him down here.'

'Rustlin'! Why, nobody could git away with it, Sontag.'

'Hell!' snorted Sad disgustedly. 'I could steal yore darn' office, and yuh wouldn't find it out for a week.'

'We ain't as bad as that, are we?'

'Worse, if such a thing is possible. You've had a train robbery, a stolen corpse, and a kidnaped lady. What have yuh done? Set around the office and cuss the heat. They come in and take a prisoner away from yuh,

185

and lock yuh in yore own jail. What have yuh done about it?'

'What can I do?' wailed Panamint. 'I'm no detective.'

'And then,' continued Sad heartlessly, 'a man is shot by rustlers – and yuh don't believe there are any rustlers. Panamint Pelley, how in hell did yuh ever get elected to office?'

'I – I got more votes than the other feller.'

'He wasn't much good, was he?'

'Not much. I don't guess he would have been any better than I am.'

'Prob'ly not. Well, let's go back and wait for the next crime. The first thing we know there'll be a killin'. They're skatin' close to murder.'

'If yo're so dam' smart, why don't you do somethin'?' flared Panamint.

'For instance?'

'Quit ridin' me, for one thing. I'm doin' my best, ain't I?'

'I reckon yuh are, and I'm sorry I rode yuh thataway, but this stuff is putting a hair edge on my temper.'

'Me, too. I'm due to bite somebody.'

They rode back to Cinco City, no wiser than when they rode out. Later on they went to see Pima, and Sad asked him how he happened to ride over to that old corral in Keno Canyon.

'I dunno,' he replied. 'I tell yuh, I've had a hunch for a long time that we was losin' cattle. The rest of the boys laughed at me – and the sheriff said I was crazy. T'day I got thinkin' I'd ride down here; and up there at the forks, somethin' told me to ride over into Keno Canyon. Next time' – he smiled wryly – 'I hope that *somethin'* keeps still. It shore led me into a lot of misery. Be lucky if I ain't crippled for life.'

The news traveled swiftly, and that night nearly all the cattlemen were in Cinco City. If there were any cattle rustlers in that country, they wanted to know about it. It was the first time anyone had been shot by an alleged rustler, and all of them respected Pima's statement, as he was an old-timer in that country. Many of them talked with Pima that evening, and with the sheriff, who tried to look wise and say little. That was Melancholy's suggestion.

'If yuh don't say anythin', they'll think yuh know somethin'.'

Sad listened to much of the conversation, but none of it was of any value to him. The boys of the JHC wanted to take Pima home with them, but the doctor advised leaving him at the hotel for a few days. Elastic Jones got drunk, as usual, celebrating the occasion. None of the Gavin outfit were in town, which gave Elastic a great talking point.

But with all the conversation, nothing constructive was done – or said. For Sad it was a disappointment, leaving him still groping in the dark for something to work on. He really believed that Pima Simpson had run into a bunch of cattle rustlers. It was the only solution he could see. But who and how was the question. Who would steal the cattle, and how dispose of them? He didn't blame the sheriff for being skeptical.

The following morning he met Panamint on his way to breakfast. The sheriff looked grimly at Sad.

'Didn't yore breakfast set good?' asked Sad.

'Breakfast set all right. Last night sometime' – Panamint hitched up his belt, spat in the dust, and grimaced sourly – 'somebody busted into Hank Fairchild's general store.'

'Yeah? And what else?'

'Ain't that enough? They took a lot of tobacco, candy, pocket-knives, a shotgun and a coupla boxes of shells. Anyway, they've missed that much.'

Sad turned with him and they went to the store. Henry Fairchild was a smallish man, with a nearly bald head and a soft voice. He showed them the broken lock on the back

188

door, where it had apparently been pried open with an iron bar.

'The bar was still here,' said Fairchild. 'The blacksmith claimed it. He said it was out behind his shop yesterday. Outside of the shotgun, the stuff we've missed ain't worth so awful much; but that shotgun was worth money. It was a sawed-off Parker, ten-gauge, and a pretty gun.'

'What kind of shells did he take?' asked Sad.

'Ten-gauge shotgun shells loaded with buckshot – two boxes. It was all I had. They took a lot of candy out of the showcase, and about a dozen pocket-knives. I dunno what else they took.'

'You could identify that shotgun?' asked the sheriff.

'Certainly. I believe it was done by tramps who dropped off the train here. Nobody around here would steal that gun – it is too well known.'

Sad nodded, but was far from convinced. Why would a tramp steal a shotgun, he asked himself. It was not a sporting arm and clumsy to carry. The choke had all been cut off the barrels, and it was only fit to shoot buckshot. Most certainly no one would hunt with a weapon of that kind. There are places where deer hunters use shotguns, but not in the Arizona hills. To Sad, a sawed-off shotgun was primarily a murderer's weapon. He had the same aversion to them that some men have toward keen-edged tools.

The sheriff was willing to accept Fairchild's theory that a tramp had stolen the stuff. Panamint was not difficult to convince.

'Who else uses a shotgun around here?' asked Sad.

'They've got one at the JHC,' replied Fairchild. 'It's a twelve-gauge. Chuck Gavin owns a twelve-gauge Winchester. I think those are the only ones. There's very little shotgun shootin' around here.'

'I hope it won't get more popular,' said Sad dryly.

Sad spent nearly all the afternoon with Old Pima, who was suffering very little, and the old man told him the history of the Cinco rangeland. Sad had an idea that the old man might give him something to think about, but except for the long-standing trouble between the JHC and the J Bar 44 there was nothing exciting later than the gold strikes fifteen miles north of Cinco City, at Aurora Borealis, now only a few tumble-down shacks. These mines had played out twelve years before, after a hectic period of about five years. Pima was of the opinion that Frank Welden had done well during the boom. He had sold several prospects at a good figure, prospects that cost him nothing.

'He was the only assayer in the country,' explained Pima, 'and maybe he discouraged prospectors into droppin' locations. Welden knows ore, that's a cinch. It shore was boomin' about that time, but it didn't last. I know of one mine Welden sold for ten thousand dollars, and there was plenty of talk that he'd salted it. Nobody could prove it. Anyway, there was more gold sunk in there than was ever taken out. There's gold quartz in these hills, but it's low-grade stuff, and yuh can't find enough. One day I found a chunk of rock out there by the JHC stable, and there was gold in sight on it. That was about three years ago. I sent to an assayer and he reported that it was worth over a thousand dollars a ton. But I never found where it came from. Probably somebody packed it down from the mines up at Aurora. They had a lot of rich stuff up there, but not enough to pay 'em.'

'Was John Cleland interested in the minin' game?' asked Sad.

'Not a bit. Old Million Dollar wouldn't know gold quartz from granite. Nope, he wasn't a bit interested.'

'Were you workin' for him at that time?'

'Oh, shore. Me and Elastic Jones have been here a long time. We drifted into this country

191

about twenty-five years ago. Cleland had been on JHC about a year. He'd jist rebuilt his ranch-house about the time we came along. We went to work for him about a year and then we drifted into Wyomin' for a summer; but we've been here ever since.'

Tom and Pete Hawker were in town that evening. They inquired if the sheriff had located Lobo Wolf and if there was anything further on the cattle rustling. Sad met them at the Cinco Saloon, but neither of them mentioned the fact that Sad and Swede had visited their ranch-house; so Sad decided that Mike Joe had been too drunk to mention it to them. Ted Bell and Larry Delago were in town that evening, and there had been a sizable poker game in progress, in which Lawyer Charley Tolman had been a heavy contributor. Sad did not play, but watched the game, and after a few rounds of the play, decided that Tom Hawker was entirely too clever with cards.

Tolman finally drew out of the game, two hundred dollars lower, accepted a drink at the bar and walked out. Sad went over to the bar and was about to engage the bartender in conversation. Tolman had stopped in the doorway to light a cigar, and then stepped out on the sidewalk.

The smashing report of a heavy gun came

from outside the saloon, and Tolman seemed fairly to spring sideways out of line with the doorway. Sad saw the flash of the gun through the thin curtain at the left-hand window. The men sprang from the poker table, as someone across the street cried out excitedly and came running.

Sad was the first man out of the saloon. The man running across the street was the sheriff, and they met at the edge of the sidewalk. Tolman was lying flat in the street, partly lighted by the saloon window.

'I saw the flash of that gun,' panted the sheriff.

'He went down the alley.'

And the sheriff was running swiftly in that direction, while Sad went round the other way, gun in hand. But there was no one in sight. They listened, but the only sound was from around on the street, so they went back. The men had carried Tolman into the saloon, but there was no need of a doctor. He had been shot with what was apparently both barrels of a shotgun, loaded with more than a dozen buckshot in each cartridge, and the range had not been over twelve or fifteen feet. Not a single shot had missed him.

The sheriff was shaky, as were most of the men in the place. Swede and Melancholy came over from the office and watched the doctor make his examination. Fairchild was there from his store.

'That stolen gun,' he said sadly. 'The only buckshot gun in the country, and they stole it to kill Tolman. Why did they kill Tolman? Tolman was only a lawyer.'

Frank Welden came after the doctor had finished examining the body, and he was badly upset. Tolman was his friend. Welden was a bit incoherent. Who would be safe now, with a maniac at large with a shotgun?

'Did Tolman have any enemies?' asked Sad.

'Enemies – no. Tolman was rather well liked. In fact, we were going to run him for prosecuting attorney next election.'

The poker game ended abruptly. The men cashed in their chips and went home. Sad went to the office with the sheriff, who was greatly upset.

'I saw the flash of that gun, Sontag; and I got over there as quick as I could. Dam' it, this is drivin' me loco, I tell yuh. Who in the devil would bush Tolman thataway? Yuh don't suppose they made a mistake in their man, do yuh? Things like that have been done.'

'I know they have,' replied Sad, but he was sure that no mistake of that kind had been made this time. Tolman had stood there in
194

the doorway long enough to light a cigar. He was wearing a gray suit and a soft black hat. No chance for anybody to confuse him with any other man in the saloon, as all of them wore cowboy garb, except the bartender and the man who was running the game.

To Sad, it was a clear case of somebody desiring to kill Tolman. They had broken into the store with the purpose of stealing that gun to kill the attorney. They didn't want any mistake in the killing, so they hit him with both barrels at short range. But why kill Tolman, wondered Sad. Tolman's law cases had never made him any bitter enemies in Cinco City; nothing to cause anyone to build up a hatred against the lawyer. In fact, Sad had mentally tagged Tolman as a man of little importance.

The sheriff paced up and down his office, swearing to himself. Things were getting worse for him every day.

'I've got a notion to resign,' he said. 'Best thing I could do, I reckon.'

'Better stick with the job,' advised Sad. 'This can't last.'

'It's lasted too long to suit me. Train-robbers, body-snatchers, burglars, jail-breakers, rustlers, and now a dam' murder. But what can I do? Yo're a hoodoo, Sontag. This country was peaceful

195

until you showed up.'

'I reckon I did put the Indian sign on things,' smiled Sad.

They held an inquest the following morning, which was merely a formality. Sad talked with Frank Welden about the murder, and decided that Welden was still frightened. His eyes were bloodshot, and he kept insisting that he did not know why anybody would want to kill Tolman.

After the inquest, Sad talked with Panamint and Melancholy. No one blamed the sheriff, but he thought they did, and flared up at Melancholy when he laughed at Panamint's arguments. He told Melancholy he could whip him on a sheepskin.

'You couldn't whip me on a quarter-section, Panamint.'

'Why fight about it?' laughed Sad. 'That don't solve anythin'. What is down in the country south of where the train was robbed?'

Panamint slumped wearily in a chair and rubbed his nose.

'Nothin' much,' replied Melancholy. 'About a mile and a half below there is what's left of the old Gonzales ranch-buildin's. They've all fell down by this time. Their springs went dry too often.'

'I've been doin' a lot of thinkin',' said Sad. 'Accordin' to what we discovered, they took

196

the body away on some kind of a rig. You say there ain't no side roads between here and Tejunga?'

'Not any. There's an old road from here to the old Gonzales ranch.'

'All right. Takin' it for granted that they used a vehicle, they had to get off that road, or go to Tejunga or Cinco City. Let's go down and take a look at the old Gonzales ranch. We'll go down the main road to where we saw them tracks beside the fence, and mebbe we can find some more of 'em down toward the ranch. It's worth a try, anyway.'

'Anythin' is worth a try,' said the sheriff. 'Saddle 'em up.'

Swede came as they went out of the office and was glad to go along. Inaction was galling to Swede.

They rode down to the spot where they found the tire tracks near the railroad fence, and then spread out, heading south. The ground was as hard as flint, but Swede discovered tire tracks three hundred yards to the southwest. The print of the hoofs showed that the horse or horses were heading northwest. They examined them closely.

'That's queer,' decided Sad. 'Don't work out right. Anyway, we'll go down to the old ranch and see what's down there.'

In a short time they came in sight of the

old ranch, and, as Melancholy said, it was in bad shape. Half of the old ranch-house was still standing, while the other half was flat on the ground, causing it to resemble an animal, rearing up to look closely at them. The two windows and the door, like two eyes and a mouth, helped out the illusion.

There was an old shed, sagging badly, and a dilapidated corral. They rode to the old house, where they dismounted. Sad immediately saw something of interest and hurried out to the old shed, where stood an old buckboard, with one front wheel missing. The old thing had been patched with baling wire, now rusted almost through. Sad examined it closely and walked out behind it toward the corral, but went back for another inspection.

'This is what they used,' he told the others. 'Look at the tires and you'll see fresh scratches from rocks. Look at that axle where the wheel is missin', it's all polished. They hid one wheel, I reckon. To keep from showin' any track, they ran it across the yard empty and by hand. It's been under that shed for a long time, and when they put it back there, mebbe in the dark, they didn't get it back exactly on the same spot. Well, that's somethin'.'

'I wonder if yo're right?' asked the sheriff anxiously.

'Shore, I'm right. That's how we found the

tracks goin' north. They brought their horses over here, hitched on to that buckboard, and took it to the railroad, pulled their job, and brought it back here. From here they had to carry that heavy casket box, and they wouldn't carry it far.'

'There ain't nothin' in the old house,' said Melancholy.

CHAPTER XII

Sad sat down on an old block of wood and looked around. He was satisfied that the men wouldn't carry that heavy box very far. The fallen end of the ranch-house offered a possible hiding-place, but Swede and Melancholy tore some of the old shack roof apart, finding nothing underneath.

There was an old root-house, the top fallen in, which did not seem to offer any possibilities, until Sad went over and took a look at it, discovering footprints in the dirt covering it.

Swede found an old broken-handled shovel, and with this they went to work, digging down to the poles, which they dragged aside. And there they discovered the top of a pine box.

There was no question about its being the casket box. The top had been unscrewed, and was only held in place with a couple of bent nails.

Inside was a plain mahogany casket, with silver handles.

'Let's take that plate off,' said Melancholy. 'It'll give us a look at the corpse, without openin' the casket.'

'That's a good idea,' agreed Sad, and Panamint quickly removed the screws with a blade of his knife, and removed the plate.

For several moments the four men stared down at the glass-covered square. Panamint was the first to speak. 'Good gosh! That ain't Cleland – it's Lobo Wolf!'

Sad Sontag sat down on a corner of the box and rolled a smoke, while the sheriff walked around in a circle, swearing at every step.

'Well,' said Sad, 'at least we know where Lobo Wolf went.'

'But where's the other body?' wailed Panamint.

'Gone where the woodbine twineth. They brought it over here, cached the box in the old root-house, and took the body away. They didn't care who found the casket. And when they killed Lobo Wolf, they put him in the casket.'

'Why would they kill Lobo Wolf?'

'Because he knew too much, and they didn't trust him. Their best bet was to murder him and have him out of the way.'

'So you think Tolman was one of the gang?'

Sad shook his head. 'As far as I can see, there was no reason for killin' Tolman. Why would anybody fear him?'

'Suppose he *knew* somethin'.'

'That's possible. But when a gang starts to killin' their own members for safety, sooner or later somebody is goin' to make a bad slip and give the whole thing away. I reckon our best move right now is to leave Melancholy and Swede here to stand guard over the remains of Lobo Wolf while me and you go to town and send a wagon out here.'

It was late in the afternoon before they brought the body to town and turned it over to the coroner. Lobo Wolf had been shot from behind and at close range. Cinco City was worried. Two murdered men at the coroner's office, and no clue to the murderers. People began looking sideways at each other. Fairchild was rather happy when he was told that Lobo Wolf had not been killed with a shotgun.

Clare was rather excited when Sad told her that the casket bore the name of a Los Angeles undertaker, although that fact did not help her case in any way. Sad told her he had given up any hope of ever finding the body of John Cleland.

'That body meant too much to them,' he explained. 'It was up to them to destroy it at once. They could have removed it there at the train, but I s'pose they were new at this corpse-stealin' game, and mebbe they kinda wanted to hide the container. Of course that casket ain't evidence, and, unless I'm mistaken, that gang is too smart to ever let us find the body of Cleland.'

Clare was badly upset over the murder of Tolman. She had been in to see Old Pima Simpson, and Pima had sworn by all the gods that the Gavins had hired somebody to kill Tolman, because Tolman was trying to help her get the JHC. It made Clare feel partly responsible.

'Old Pima is crazy,' declared Sad. 'It's that old enmity. I doubt if the Gavins ever knew Tolman was yore lawyer. Anyway, Tolman didn't do much toward helpin' yore case, Clare; and as far as yore responsibility – shucks! Tolman took the case, knowin' all its bad points – *and he never stopped them two loads of buckshot on that account.*'

'Are you sure of that, Sad?'

'Just as sure as I'm talkin' to you. Pima's

theory is ridiculous. If Tolman had evidence to prove yore case, and they knew it, I'd agree with Pima.'

'Perhaps he had discovered something.'

'You can't argue with me,' said Sad, grinning. 'Lobo Wolf was one of the gang. He and another man tried to steal that will from yuh, and Lobo got caught. Because they were afraid he'd talk, they broke jail, took him out and killed him, sealin' his lips forever. As an afterthought, they stole you, hid yuh in Gavin's stable, throwin' the evidence against the J Bar 44.'

'Oh, I hope you're right, Sad.'

'It's a cinch. The Gavin family are not fools. Only fools would hide yuh in a hayloft. A kid would know better than that.'

'You don't think they'd harm me, do you?' she asked anxiously.

'Not now. You don't know anythin' to harm them.'

'Aren't you afraid?'

'Scared stiff. No, I'm not jokin' – it's too serious for jokes. Before tomorrow every man on this range will know that I was the one who found that casket and the body of Lobo Wolf. Murderers scare easy, Clare. They know they are in the shadow of the rope, and they'll keep on killin' to save themselves. But' – Sad smiled coldly – 'I shore hope some of

203

'em make a foolish break before they get around to me.'

'Oh, I hope they don't harm anybody again.'

'I hope not – but they will.'

The town was quiet that evening. Tom Hawker and his brother came in, as did the boys from the JHC, but none of them stayed late. It seemed to Sad that everybody in the country was worried. Even the sheriff kept looking behind himself – and admitted it. Sad and Swede went to bed early and talked things over. Swede wanted to pull out.

'They're afraid of us now, Sad,' he argued, 'and don't yuh ever forget that one of 'em uses a buckshot-shooter. That don't give yuh a even break.'

'We can't quit now, Swede. Somebody has got to clean up that bunch, and it might as well be us. If the Big Book has our name connected with this deal, we've got to go through. Don't the Bible say, "The son of man goeth as it is written of him." It's that old movin' finger that Omar wrote about. Shucks, we've been in tight places before. I'm jist commencin' to see a light. It ain't very bright, but it's – what's all that yellin'?'

The town was as quiet as a tomb, and the voice came quavering. It was like the far-off voice from a phonograph – *'Fire! Fire! Fi-i-i-i-i-ire!'*

Swede sprang out of bed and ran to their window, which fronted on the main street. There was no sign of fire in that direction. Across the street and a little farther south were the lighted windows of the Cinco Saloon, but tonight there was no line of horses at the hitch-rack. A man came out of the saloon and stood on the edge of the sidewalk. Farther down the street someone spoke loudly, and the man went running in that direction. There were more voices now, and one man bellowed, 'Fire! Shake a leg, will yuh? *Fi-i-i-i-ire!'*

Sad was climbing into his clothes in the dark, and Swede came from the window to join him. Hastily they pulled on their clothes and went running down the stairs. The hotel-keeper was just going out, and he called to them that it was Frank Welden's home.

They had seen his place, a modest cottage on the east side of town, where an old lady kept house for him. Cinco City came piling out to see the fire, which was roaring through the tinder-dry frame structure, and by the time Sad and Swede arrived, there was no chance to save any of it. Smoke and flame were pouring out through the windows and a few minutes later the whole roof was a mass of flames.

They had barely arrived when Frank Welden and Henry Fairchild came. Welden said he had been spending the evening at Fairchild's home. The sheriff had Mrs. Beetson, Welden's housekeeper, with him, and Sad listened while she told Welden what had happened.

'I was just getting ready for bed when I heard a crackling noise. It did sound like fire, but I didn't think it could be. I knew there was no fire in the kitchen stove, but I went out there, and the kitchen was full of smoke, which seemed to be coming from the back porch. I opened the door and the flames came right in at me.

'Well, I ran through the house and went out the front door. I ran around toward the back of the house, and in the light of the fire I saw a man. He was out there, standing still, and I think he had a gun in his hands. I called to him to help me, but he didn't move or say anything, and when I began calling real loud, he turned and ran away.'

'My God!' said Welden hoarsely, and his face went white in the light of the flames.

'I feel sure somebody set fire to the house,' quavered the old lady. 'I'm sure it didn't accidentally catch fire.'

Frank Welden shook his head slowly and turned away from the fire. There was nothing to be done toward putting it out. Already the roof was about to fall in. Even the little picket fence was blazing in spots. Luckily there were no houses near enough to catch fire from the showering brands. In a few minutes more the walls began caving in, followed by the roof, which sent up a towering flood of sparks and burning brands.

Sad and Swede went back to the hotel. Clare had watched it from her window, and Sad told her whose home it was, but he didn't tell her that someone had set the house on fire.

'What do yuh make of it?' asked Swede, when they were back in bed.

'Make of it? If Frank Welden had been at home, he'd be in the morgue right now. The dirty murderer fired the house, expecting to draw Welden around to the fire, where he'd load him full of lead. Mebbe they can't take a chance at Welden in the daylight.'

Swede whistled softly. 'Somebody's gunnin' for the banker, eh? Well, you've got to give 'em credit for mixin' their victims. Punchers, lawyers, Injuns, and bankers all look alike to 'em. I wonder if that same gang didn't kill old man Cleland?'

'Swede,' said Sad sleepily, 'once in a while you show almost human intelligence. Good-night.'

207

'Good-night,' yawned Swede. 'I s'pose we may as well say our prayers.'

'Go ahead – but mention no names. This place is gettin' spooky.'

Sad Sontag and Melancholy Day, deputy Sheriff of Cinco City, sat together in front of the sheriff's office. It was about noon, the day after Lobo Wolf's body had been discovered.

'I dunno whatsa use of holdin' inquests,' said Melancholy sadly. 'Go to a lotta trouble, testify to things we already know about, and decide that Lobo Wolf came to his death from a gunshot wound inflicted by persons unknown. Same old cut-and-dried tripe. And the feller who shot him is prob'ly on the jury. That's the hell of it, Sontag – yuh don't know who's who in this danged country.'

'She's a spooky range,' agreed Sad. 'Plenty spooky.'

'For instance,' said Melancholy, looking up the street, 'why use six punchers to herd a coupla cows and their offsprings?'

'Don't look fair to the cows,' smiled Sad.

But such was a fact. Closer inspection proved it to be Bat Gavin, Chuck Gavin, Dick Ellers, Bud McCoy, Dan McKenna, and Scotty Gleason, every man on the J Bar 44, except Casey Jones, the Chinese cook. They rode in close to the two red cows and their small offspring, and swung them in to the sidewalk in front of Sad and Melancholy.

Bat Gavin and his men merely nodded – not a smile in the crowd. Bat Gavin dismounted and came around to the sidewalk.

'Where's Panamint?' he asked.

'Eatin' his dinner,' replied the deputy. 'Whatsa matter, Bat?'

'Matter enough. Look at them calves.'

One little red calf swung its right side around and on his hip was the J Bar 44 brand, freshly burned, looking greatly oversize on the little animal. Melancholy glanced at the red cow's left side, and on the hip was burned a circle dot at least a foot across. Melancholy whistled softly and examined the other cow and calf. They were marked the same. The J Bar 44 men watched Melancholy gravely as he turned from the animals, leaned one shoulder against a porch-post, and scratched his head foolishly.

'Well?' drawled Bat Gavin harshly.

'Well?' echoed Melancholy. 'If anybody was to ask me, I'd say that somebody done vented a Circle Dot and run on the J Bar 44.'

'Looks that way, don't it?'

'Beyond the shadder of a doubt. The Circle Dot brands on the left hip, and they're the only ones what brand there. Them are Circle Dot cows, but their babies shore look plenty J Bar 44 to me.'

Sad glanced up to see Ted Bell, Larry Delago, and Mose Heilman coming toward them, accompanied by the sheriff. They had all been at the restaurant. Bat Gavin saw them, and waited for Melancholy to explain to the sheriff, who made an examination, while the JHC cowboys stood together on the sidewalk, making no comments.

'What's the answer, Bat?' queried the sheriff.

'The answer is that somebody has been tryin' to put the deadwood on my outfit. Things have been hinted around about me and my gang havin' something to do with the killin' of John Cleland. Yuh thought I stole that girl, and yuh think I had somethin' to do with that jail-break. Well, go ahead and think what yuh please about them things – we don't care a dam'. But I jist want to say that the man who run my iron on them calves is a dirty skunk of a coward.'

He turned and looked at Ted Bell and his two men.

'Bell, some of yore outfit talk too much. I hear that you hinted me and my gang smoked up Pima Simpson. That's a dam' lie. Roll that in a weed and smoke it, will yuh? Some of yuh have hinted that the J Bar 44 rustled JHC cows. That's another dirty lie. Smoke that one, will yuh? And lemme tell yuh another
210

thing: the first time one of yore outfit makes a crack about me and mine, I'll come over and move yore dam' outfit off the Cinco range. That's my talk and it's on the square. It's yore turn now.'

Ted Bell's face was red, his eyes snapping, but he shut his lips tightly. He was wise enough to keep still. Six to three, all aching for trouble. Bell knew it would be suicide to start anything with that outfit. He spoke to his two men and they went away without a word. Bat Gavin looked after them until they entered the Cinco City Saloon, and turned back to the sheriff.

'Them calves are worth about five dollars apiece,' he said slowly, as he reached in his pocket and brought out some money, which he handed to the sheriff.

'Here's fifteen dollars, at seven-fifty apiece, Panamint. You give this to Bill Haskell, and explain what happened. I'll fatten them calves at the ranch and eat veal later on.'

The sheriff took the money and put it in his pocket.

'That's square of yuh, Bat,' he said.

'I want to be square with everybody,' bitterly, 'and all I ask is a square deal in return.'

'Yo're entitled to one, Bat.'

'I'm glad somebody thinks so. Dick, will

211

you and the boys haze them critters off the main street?'

'I think Uncle Billy will be in today,' said the sheriff. 'They mostly do come in on Saturday, and I'll explain things to him.'

'Thank yuh, Panamint. It's lucky we found them cows. Things like that are hard to explain away, yuh know, except that it was so dam' foolish. Nobody but a half-wit would do a thing like that.'

Bat Gavin nodded pleasantly to Sad, and Chuck smiled as they turned and rode back up the street, where they dismounted and tied their horses at the rack in front of Fairchild's store.

'Didn't old Bat tell Ted Bell where to head in at,' chuckled Melancholy. 'And Ted took it like a little man.'

'Pretty big odds,' smiled Sad, and they walked back into the office, where they sat down.

There were several sheets of paper on the sheriff's desk, and Sad picked up one of them, as he tilted back in his chair against the wall, listening to the sheriff and deputy arguing over what had just occurred. Sad folded the paper to fit an envelope, unfolding and folding it a number of times, creasing it tightly each time, until it was slightly soiled. Finally he put it in a side pocket of

212

his trousers and rolled a smoke.

The inquest over Lobo Wolf's body was scheduled for that afternoon, and the sheriff told Sad that he and Swede would be obliged to testify.

'We're used to it,' smiled Sad.

The sheriff picked up his hat, and Sad followed him outside.

'Will yuh do me a favor?' asked Sad.

'Shore will.'

Sad took Cleland's will from his pocket and showed it to Panamint.

'Take a good look at that signature, will yuh?'

'All right: what about it?'

'We'll go up to the bank and I want you to ask Welden to let us see that same letter he showed me the other day – the one from Cleland. I want yore opinion on that signature. Yuh might also ask him to let us see the signature on that mortgage against the JHC.'

'Shore, I'll ask him.'

Welden did not seem surprised, and let them have the letter from his files. The three of them looked it over, but Sad did not mention the will to Welden.

'Does the signature on the mortgage correspond to this one?' asked Sad.

'Certainly. I'll show it to you.'

213

Welden secured the mortgage from the safe and let them see the signature. It appeared identical with the one on the letter. Welden replaced the mortgage and Sad gave him back the folded letter, which was put in the files.

'Anything new?' asked Welden.

'Not a dam' thing,' growled the sheriff. Sad thanked Welden and they went out together.

'Anythin' else?' asked the sheriff.

'No, I reckon that's all; and thanks.'

They went back to the sheriff's office, and Sad sat down with the brand register, which showed all the registered brands in the State. He studied the brands of the local range closely. Suddenly he snorted aloud, blowing all the tobacco out of his cigarette, the brown paper fluttering on his lip. The sheriff looked curiously at him, wondering at the expression on Sad's lean face as he leaned forward, staring into space.

He got to his feet and walked to the doorway, where he stood, leaning against one shoulder, looking up the street.

'What in hell hit you?' asked the sheriff.

Sad laughed shortly, but did not answer. The sheriff picked up the register, which Sad had let drop to the floor beside his chair, and placed it on the desk. He turned to Sad and was about to repeat his question, but Sad was

214

singing softly and not very musically a version of Badger Clark's poem:

'Way up high in the Muggy-owns, if you ever
come there at night,
You'll hear a ruckus among the stones that'll lift
yore hair with fright;
You'll see a cow-hoss thunder by and a lion trail
along,
And the rider bold, with chin on high, sings forth
his glory song:
'Oh, glory be to me,' says he, 'and to my mighty
noose!
Oh, pardner, tell my friends below I took a ragin'
dream in tow,
And if I didn't lay him low – I never turned
him loose.'

'Yuh must be happy,' grunted the sheriff.

Sad started and looked around.

'Eh?' he grunted.

'You was singin'.'

'I was – yuh say I was? Panamint, yo're the first man I ever met who had a real ear for music.'

He walked away from the office, still humming a verse of 'High-Chin Bob,' and strolled up toward the hotel. Swede and Melancholy drifted around to the office in a

215

little while and asked for Sad.

'The last I seen of him, he was goin' up the street, kinda singin' to himself,' replied the sheriff.

'Singin'?'

'Well, he was makin' a noise over some words.'

Swede took a deep breath and hitched up his belt.

'Singin', eh?'

'Ain't he got no right to sing?' asked Melancholy.

'Yea-a-ah, I s'pose. But any time he starts singin', he's found out –' and Swede went striding up toward the hotel.

'Both of 'em crazy as bedbugs,' grunted the sheriff. 'Sontag was readin' the brand register, and all to once he grunted like a man that's been hit in the belly. He lets the book slide to the floor, gets up and leans against the side of the door, where he busts into song. Crazy actions.'

'Well,' sighed Melancholy, 'we're all more or less crazy. If somethin' don't break pretty soon, we'll be more.'

Frank Welden had been doing considerable wondering about Sontag's interest in the case. In fact, Welden's nerves were in bad shape. There was no question in his mind that someone had purposely burned his house

216

and that the person had intended loading his body with lead slugs. With his home only an ash-heap, and the knowledge that someone was intending to kill him, the immediate future was anything but rose-tinted.

Welden had never considered Panamint Pelley as a brainy man. In fact, he had always considered the sheriff as a brave man who didn't have brains enough to make him inquisitive. But Sontag was a different proposition. Welden rubbed his lean jaw reflectively. He was going to foreclose on the JHC right away. Charley Tolman had handled the legal affairs of the bank, but he was dead, and Welden would have to find another lawyer. Welden wondered if the murderer of Tolman was the same man who fired his house.

And why did Sontag and the sheriff want to see those signatures? he wondered. Finally he went to the safe and took out the mortgage, which he spread out on his desk.

'I wonder just why they compared those signatures,' he muttered to himself, as he went to the files and got the letter from John Cleland.

Seating himself at the desk, he unfolded the letter. Suddenly he grunted softly to himself, a queer expression in his eyes. The paper was blank. Quickly he went back to the files, searching swiftly. But there was no mistake. The letter was gone and in its place was the blank paper, folded the same as the missing letter had been.

CHAPTER XIII

Welden sat down at his desk, staring at the blank paper. What did it mean? he wondered. Who was this Sad Sontag, and why did he steal that letter? Of what value would that letter be to him? He jerked up suddenly, as someone came in. It was Ted Bell.

'Hello, Frank,' he said curtly. 'What's the matter – you look sour.'

Welden smiled grimly and came over to the railing, where he rested his elbows.

'What do you know about Sad Sontag, Ted?' he asked.

'Not a dam' thing.' Bell had been drinking.

'Ted, did you ever get a letter from John Cleland?'

'Nope. I've told you several times –'

'I know.'

'What about it?'

'Could you swear to his signature?'

'Well, you've got it on a letter and –'

218

'Did have,' dryly. 'Oh, I've got the mortgage, but awhile ago Sontag and Panamint came in. They wanted to see the signatures on the letter and on the mortgage. I let 'em look at both. Awhile ago I looked for that letter, and here's what I found in its place.'

He handed Bell the blank sheet of paper.

'One of them kept the letter and slipped me this folded sheet.'

Bell's eyes narrowed, as he looked at the banker.

'What's the idea?' he asked coldly.

Welden shook his head. 'I don't know.'

'What's all this talk about somebody settin' fire to yore home, and tryin' to kill you off, Frank?'

Welden's fingers trembled as he folded the sheet of paper.

'The house burned to the ground, and the old lady says there was a man who had a gun.'

'The same man who killed Tolman?'

'I don't know who killed Tolman – do you?'

'I wish I did. But what about this stolen letter? What good –'

'That's just it. Did you see the signature on the will?'

'Nope.'

219

'I did; and it wasn't much like the signature on that letter.'

'Which one got it?'

'I think it was Sontag.'

'He's pretty thick with that girl.'

'Tolman advised her to drop the case.'

'Well, she's still here. I reckon Tolman's advice didn't take.'

'She's a fool. I'm going to foreclose on that mortgage right away.'

'Uh-huh. You better hang onto yore nerve – you looked scared.'

Welden took the mortgage back to the safe, and Ted Bell went out. The foreman of the JHC was still smarting from what Bat Gavin had told him, and was in the proper mood to start trouble with somebody. He noticed that the J Bar 44 horses were missing from the hitch-rack, and decided they had gone home. He didn't notice that Chuck Gavin had moved his horse to the Cinco Saloon rack.

Bell stopped in front of the hotel to roll a cigarette. His last few drinks of whiskey were taking effect, and he felt exhilarated. In fact, he was a little disappointed that the Gavin outfit had gone home

Larry Delago and Mose Heilman came from the Cinco Saloon and asked him if he was going to attend the inquest over the body of Lobo Wolf. Bell shook his head, and the two men went on together toward the courthouse. Tom Hawker and Mike Joe rode in and tied their horses at the Cinco rack. They were in for the inquest, and Bell waited for them to cross the street.

'What's new, Tom?' he asked, as they came up to him.

Hawker shook his head as he stepped in close and said to Bell: 'I was kinda curious to know somethin' about Sontag. They said he was an old friend of Buck Hogan, down at the Sawbuck outfit; so I took a run down there. Buck is in the East with a train of cows, but I got plenty second-hand information from the boys, who have heard Buck talk about Sontag. Accordin' to Buck's talk, Sontag is the slickest cattle detective on earth.'

Ted Bell's eyebrows lifted quickly.

'Detective, eh?'

'Plenty.'

'Huh!' thoughtfully. 'Workin' for the express company on that robbery, eh?'

'*Quien sabe?*'

Bell shoved his hand deep in his pockets and leaned the point of his right shoulder against a post.

'Well, that's all right with me,' he said. 'Are yuh goin' to the inquest?'

'Shore. Lobo was one of my men.'

'Lobo dead,' said Mike Joe flatly.

221

Ted Bell laughed shortly, eyeing the Indian. 'Dead, eh?'

'Deader'n hell.'

'Yeah, I s'pose he is.'

Hawker and Bell grinned at each other, and the two men from the Tomahawk went down toward the courthouse.

'Dam' Injun!' snorted Ted Bell disgustedly. He turned his head and looked at the hotel entrance. He knew Clare was living there. Bell had never been much of a hand with the ladies, except the dance-hall kind, but now he had an idea that he would like to talk with Clare. At least, it would kill time until after the inquest. He adjusted his neckerchief, placed his hat at a rakish angle, and walked into the cool, dark lobby of the little hotel.

He was a little blinded by the change of light, and stopped short of the desk. He was conscious of somebody near him, and as quick as his eyes were focused to the change, he saw Clare and Chuck Gavin seated near the wall, close together. They were looking at him curiously, but did not speak. He looked around, as though expecting someone else in there, turned on his heel and walked out again. Just outside the doorway he laughed aloud, and went across to the Cinco Saloon, where only the bartender was left, as everyone else had gone to the inquest.

222

'Somethin' funny happened?' asked the bartender.

'Shore was funny. Let's me and you have a drink.'

The inquest over the remains of Lobo Wolf was by no means 'a cut-and-dried affair.' Except that there was no prisoner, it resembled a real trial. Sad's testimony, in which he told of discovering the wheel-tracks, tracing them to the old ranch, and later uncovering the body of Lobo Wolf in a casket, was of interest to everybody in the room. Even the prosecuting attorney questioned Sad, asking him to repeat what had happened, that night when he had shot Lobo Wolf in the hotel.

'In your opinion, why did Lobo Wolf and his companion try to rob Miss Nolan that night?' he asked Sad.

'To steal John H. Cleland's will.'

'I have never seen the will,' admitted the lawyer, 'but I have been told it is not Cleland's writing. That is, it is not his signature.'

'Somebody thinks it is,' smiled Sad, and the crowd laughed with him.

'Have you any opinion why Lobo Wolf was killed?'

'To shut his mouth.'

'To shut his mouth? For what reason?'

'Lobo was afraid of goin' to prison, and

223

he would tell what he knew to save himself. They knew he'd talk; so they took him out and killed him.'

The lawyer nodded slowly. 'I think that is right. I talked with him, and he was afraid. In fact' – he turned to the crowd – 'I offered him clemency if he would tell who hired him.'

The six-man jury brought in the usual verdict and the inquest was over. The prosecuting attorney, sheriff, and Sontag talked things over after the crowd was gone.

'It is a damnable situation,' said the lawyer.

'As far as we know, some of that jury might have been the ones who killed Lobo Wolf. One of them might have been the man who fired Welden's home.'

'It shore does complicate things,' grinned Sad. He took an envelope from his pocket and looked at a penciled address.

'How well do yuh know the telegraph operator here?' he asked the sheriff.

'Pretty good.'

Sad took a piece of paper from the judge's desk and wrote a few words beneath the address which he copied from the envelope. he showed it to the sheriff, who read it aloud to the lawyer.

HAROLD WELDEN,
FIGUEROA BUILDING,

LOS ANGELES, CALIF.
COME AT ONCE, NEED ADVICE.

FRANK

'I want yuh to send that telegram right away,'
said Sad. 'And I want you to instruct the
operator to hold any telegrams for Frank
Welden until we can look 'em over.'

'What's the idea?' asked the sheriff.

'I can't tell yuh yet. It can't hurt anybody,
and it might help a little. Harold Welden is a
brother of Frank Welden, yuh know.'

'But what does the telegram mean?' queried
the attorney.

'To get him out here. Harold Welden knew
John Cleland, and was at Cleland's home
shortly after Cleland was killed, but refuses to
state that the body was that of Cleland when
Tolman wired for identification. Unless I'm
mistaken Harold Welden will come along like
a nice little boy, possibly wiring Frank that he
is comin'. And we want to stop that wire.'

'I'll do it,' said the sheriff. 'I'll do anythin'
– for a change.'

Sad went across the street to the Cinco
City Saloon, where nearly everyone had gone
following the inquest. Melancholy and Swede
were busy at a pool-table, as usual. Ted Bell
and his two men were at the bar, and Ted was
laughing over something. Sad could see he

225

was drunk enough to be recklessly insolent. He eyed Sad closely and seemed about to say something, when Larry Delago touched him on the arm, as though drawing his attention to Chuck Gavin, who was coming in.

Ted Bell turned his head and looked at Chuck, who paid no attention to him, but Bell was not to be denied. He smashed his fist down on the bar, causing the glasses to dance drunkenly.

'Ladies and gentlemen!' roared Bell. 'We have with us this evenin' –'

He indicated with a wave of his hand, drawing the attention of the room to the young man from the J Bar 44. Chuck stopped and his eyes narrowed, but he said nothing.

'Mr. Chuck Gavin, the salty young gent from the J Bar 44,' continued Bell insolently. Possibly he felt safe as only one of the Gavin outfit was present.

A man stepped out of line with the two men, and the bartender hastened to the other end of the bar. Even Larry Delago slid along the bar, playing safe. The games all stopped and conversation ceased.

'Yuh can't hardly beat the Gavin family,' said Ted Bell. 'They'd do anythin' to get that water from the JHC. They even tried to buy out that female from Los Angeles who thinks she inherited the ranch, but when they found out she couldn't sell it, even if she did get it, they're tryin' to marry her into the Gavin family. That's schemin' for yuh.'

Ted Bell laughed foolishly, triumphantly, but his laughter died quickly. Chuck Gavin was leaning forward facing Bell, his right elbow crooked, his right hand flexing over the butt of his holstered gun. There was a world of menace in those clutching fingers, apparently itching to flash down and grip the black handle of that big Colt. But no one was watching the hand; it was the face of the man they were watching. All trace of youth was gone. Nothing was left but the gray mask, a line for a mouth, and eyes so nearly closed that they seemed but glittering slits.

Bell's drunkenness seemed to vanish. His mouth sagged a little and he did not know what to do with his hands.

'You can tell 'em all – that's a lie,' said Chuck, and his voice was as cold as steel on a zero morning.

Ted Bell's face twisted. He wanted to do something, say something. Perhaps he was the equal of Chuck Gavin with a gun, but –

'Tell 'em yuh lie,' said Chuck. 'I'm waitin'.'

Ted Bell mastered his vocal cords at last.

'All r-right – mebby I was mistaken.'

It was an effort for Bell to talk.

'Tell 'em yuh lied,' said Chuck.

Ted swallowed heavily. 'I – I said –'

'You said mebby yuh was mistaken. Yo're a dirty liar, Bell, and I want yuh to admit it. Go ahead, you coyote pup.'

Bell nodded, swallowed heavily.

'I lied,' he admitted painfully.

Chuck backed slowly to the doorway and went outside. He had no more than disappeared when Bell cursed softly and started for the door, but he was blocked by Sad Sontag, bumped aside, and was obliged to grasp at a table for support. He whirled quickly, facing Sad.

'Get to hell out of my way, will yuh?' snapped Bell angrily.

'Go back to the bar and behave yourself,' said Sad coldly. 'When a man eats crow, he can't kick if the bones hurt his stummick.'

'Dam' you, this ain't none of yore business!'

'I'll make it my business. Gavin made yuh crawl on yore belly, and I'm not goin' to see yuh shootin' at his back. Go over to the bar and git the liquor back that soaked through yore pores when he made yuh crawl.'

Ted Bell looked squarely in Sad's gray eyes, and he saw something that told him to be a good boy. Reluctantly, swearing under his breath, he went back to the bar. Larry Delago and Mose Heilman eyed Sad with disfavor, but said nothing as Sad went back to the pool-table, where Swede was leaning on his cue, one hand resting on his belt.

'Good boy,' said Swede softly. 'That's tellin' 'em. I had them two at the bar all lined up, but they never lifted a hand.'

Ted Bell and his two men had a drink, and walked out together. The crowd in the salon was rather amused. Tom Hawker seemed to study Sad quite closely, as though weighing him in a mental balance. Mike Joe, humped in a chair against the wall, watched Sad with lack-luster eyes, and, when the lanky cowboy caught his eye, the Indian smiled a little. Sad smiled back at him, but the Indian turned his head away.

Sad and Swede were eating supper in the Chinese restaurant that evening when the sheriff came in and sat down with them. There were several others in the place, but during the meal the sheriff slid a telegram across the table to Sad. It was directed to Frank Welden, and read:

LEAVING HERE TONIGHT

HAL

'Good stuff,' chuckled Sad, pocketing the telegram. 'The agent won't tell Welden, will he?'

'Not a chance. All he asks is that I

229

protect him, in case Welden finds it out and complains to the company.'

'He won't need to worry about that.'

It was about ten o'clock that evening when Sad went over to the hotel and met Clare in the hallway. She had been visiting with Mrs. Fairchild, who had invited her over for the evening, and was in good spirits.

'I was wonderin' if I could talk awhile with you,' said Sad.

'Why, certainly.'

Clare lighted the lamp in her room and they sat down together. She had heard what had happened in the Cinco Saloon that afternoon, but questioned Sad about the details.

'Oh, I'm sorry they quarreled about me,' she said.

'Don't let that bother yuh, Clare. I want to ask a few questions. Did you ever doubt that John Cleland wrote that will?'

'Why should I doubt it?'

'Was you familiar with his writin'?'

'No. You see, he wrote very little. In fact, I used to write letters for him on my typewriter, because he often said that no one could read his writing after it got cold.'

Sad smiled as he took the stolen letter from his pocket, unfolded it, and handed it to her.

'Did you write that?'

Clare looked at it closely and smiled at Sad.

'Of course I wrote it. I remember it very well.'

Sad leaned forward in his chair, looking at her intently.

'Is that his signature, Clare?'

She laughed and shook her head.

'I signed his name. Why, I've signed lots of letters for him. He said I signed his name plainer than he could, and – what's the matter?'

Sad's lips were laughing, but his eyes were hard as flint.

'Are yuh sure, Clare? Don't make any mistakes in this.'

'Of course, I'm sure. I know my own writing.'

A door closed softly and someone was going down the hallway. Sad listened until the footsteps died away down the stairs.

'Yuh can hear every word in this place,' he said softly. 'I hope nobody heard what was said.'

He opened the door and looked down the hall, but there was no one in sight; so he came back and sat down.

'Mrs. Fairchild says that everyone is nervous around here,' said Clare. 'Mrs. Beetson, who kept house for Mr. Welden, was over to see Mrs. Fairchild today, and she swears she saw a man with a gun, watching the

231

house start burning, and when she called him, he ran away.'

'Where is Welden livin' now?'

'Here in this hotel.'

Sad got quickly to his feet. 'Do yuh know which room?'

'I haven't any idea.'

Sad went over to the door, where he stopped and said:

'Lock this door tight and leave the key half-turned in the lock. We can't take any more chances now. I'll see yuh later.'

Clare locked the door behind him, and Sad went downstairs, where he found the hotel man sprawled in a chair, smoking a pipe.

'Well, what's goin' to happen tonight?' he asked.

'I dunno,' smiled Sad. 'That's hard to tell. Is Frank Welden goin' to live here at the hotel?'

'For a while, I reckon.'

'What room did he take?'

'Number ten.'

Sad lighted a cigarette and strolled outside. Frank Welden's room was next to Clare's, and there was only a thin partition between. The hotel man came and stood in the doorway.

'Welden jist went out awhile ago,' he said. 'If I was him, I'd shore stay under cover.'

'That's right,' laughed Sad. He sauntered

down the street, crossed over to the other side, and entered the livery stable. The stableman grinned at him as he went into a stall to talk to his horse. The stableman came over and leaned against the stall.

'I'll betcha that's some bronc,' he said. 'Got a lotta sense.'

'Yeah, he's pretty wise. How long ago did Welden leave?'

'Welden? Oh, mebby fifteen minutes ago.'

'Did he say where he was goin'?'

'Didn't say. Just for a ride, I reckon. He ain't been ridin' much lately. Used to ride quite a lot, but never had a horse of his own. I reckon the loss of his house made him feel bad, 'cause he shore is nervous.'

'Too bad he lost his house.'

'Ain't it? I wonder if somebody was gunnin' for him? Prob'ly the old lady imagined it.'

'Prob'ly.'

Sad went back to the hotel, wondering where Welden had gone. He felt sure that Welden had heard what Clare said about that signature. Swede was in the lobby, and when they went to their rooms, Sad told him about it.

'Well, that'll cook Mr. Welden's goose, eh?' grinned Swede.

'That part of it is all right, Swede; but that's only half of it. We've got to put the

233

deadwood where it belongs before we start blowin' a horn. Right now we're in bad shape. Welden may not have any part in the rest of the deviltry, but I'm bettin' he's crooked as a snake in a cactus patch, and right now he's a scared crook, which makes him as dangerous as a cornered coyote. He thinks we've got him where the hair is short.'

'Well, ain't yuh?'

'Not yet. I'm still workin' where the hair is long, but she's gettin' shorter every day. But keep yore eyes peeled, 'cause unless I'm mistaken, the fuse is also gettin' shorter.'

'Who'll I keep my eyes peeled for?'

'Don't trust anybody.'

'I was in to see Pima Simpson today. He wants to go back to the ranch, and the doctor says he'll be able to go pretty soon. He still insists that the Gavin family are the ones who shot him, and he's anxious to get well and take a crack at some of 'em.'

'He's safer in bed. The Gavins might be unhealthy folks to shoot at. I can't say about the others, but I'd never choose Chuck Gavin. That kid is a gunfighter. Man, how he did shrink Ted Bell! They may be a tough outfit, but I'd like to have 'em backin' my side in a fight. I wish I knew who stole that shotgun from the store, 'cause I hate to be flinchin' all the time. You've got a chance against a

234

bullet, but when they start sprayin' buckshot – well –' Sad yanked savagely at a boot – 'there's no use dodgin'. I only hope there ain't an entry opposite my name in the big Book, which says, "Load of buckshot from a riot gun in a town called Cinco City."'

'The manner of death don't make no difference, does it?'

'It does to me, Swede. I want 'em to say, "Don't he look natural?" instead of sayin', "Ain't he a mess?" Is that door locked? Better be sure.'

'Scared.'

'Well, if I ain't, I don't know the feelin'.'

Sad was a light sleeper, and he heard Frank Welden come back. After he was in his room, Sad lighted a match and looked at his watch. It showed a few minutes of two o'clock.

'Well,' decided Sad, 'he had plenty time to go a long ways.'

CHAPTER XIV

The next morning Sad and Swede saddled their horses and rode out of Cinco City at daylight. The town was fast asleep, and they went out quietly, heading toward the JHC.

235

Judging from the smoking stovepipe, Old Elastic Jones was cooking breakfast as they dismounted near the top of a small ridge and watched the JHC ranch-house.

They saw three cowboys go from the bunkhouse to the kitchen, and in about half an hour the same cowboys went to the stable, where they saddled their horses and rode away, going east. The sun was getting hot by the time Sad and Swede mounted and rode down to the ranch-house, where Elastic Jones greeted them heartily.

'C'mon in and have some breakfast. C'mon in and I'll fry yuh a aig. What's new in the city of crime? Nobody killed last night? Huh! Whatsa matter with 'em – slowin' up?'

'Yuh can't expect a man for breakfast every mornin',' laughed Sad. 'We're civilized.'

'How long since? Civilized, hell! How's Pima?'

'I seen him yesterday,' said Swede. 'He's doin' fine.'

'Couldn't kill him with a pickaxe, and I shore miss him,' sighed Elastic. 'Me and him have been together a long time. Fight alla time, but neither of us means it. I wish he'd come back here. Last time I talked with him he asked me if I'd help him clean up the Gavins, and I said I would. Feller has to say 'most anythin' to a sick man. Straight up or over?'

'Straight up for both,' smiled Sad.

'Ted Bell allus wants hot grease over his yolk. Makes it look to me like a blind eye. What's new?'

'Nothin' much.'

'I don't git as much news as I did before Pima went sour on things. He used to bring me all the news. The rest of the gang don't seem to think I want to keep posted. Larry did come off his high hoss far enough to tell me about the inquest. Grab a chair and I'll pile up the grub.'

'What time did Welden come out here last night?' asked Sad, as he attacked his breakfast.

'Frank Welden?'

'Yeh – the banker.'

'He wasn't here – not that I know about.'

'You sleep here in the house, don'tcha?'

'Yeah. Me and Pima bunk up here.'

'The rest bunk down below, eh?'

'Yeah. Ted Bell used to sleep here, but he don't no more. Welden might have been here, but nobody mentioned it to me. Ted said that Welden was going to foreclose his mortgage on this place, and he said we'd soon be workin' for the Cinco City Bank. I don't care a dam'. How's the aigs?'

'Best I ever ate,' declared Sad. 'You shore

237

can cook 'em.'

'Best cook between the Poles, if I do say it myself. How about a couple more of them cackleberries, eh?'

'Four is all I ever ate for breakfast,' said Sad.

'Uh-huh. Have trouble with yore stummick?'

'Nope. Four eggs kinda kills my appetite.'

'Some folks do have delicate appetites thataway. Do yuh know' – fanning a fly off his nose – 'I never knowed you was a detective.'

Sad looked up quickly, his mouth full of food.

'You don't look like no detective to me,' continued Elastic. 'But I don't reckon many detectives do. I heard Ted Bell tellin' Larry Delago – they was out on the back porch – that Tom Hawker heard all about you down at the Sawbuck Ranch in the Sweetwater. Do you know Buck Hogan?'

'Yeah, I know Buck,' slowly.

'Ted said Buck went East with some cows, but Tom found out all about you down at the Sawbuck.'

'Said I was a detective, eh?'

'Yea-a-ah. How about a little more bacon? No? Biscuits? Good for yore stummick. Plenty sody in 'em. Said yuh was detectin'' train-robbers.'

'I didn't know Tom Hawker had been down to the Sawbuck.'

'I guess he was. Coffee? Canned cow over there. I hope I live to work on a ranch where they have real cow milk. Not that I ever use the dam' wishy-washy stuff – but it's the principle of the thing. Yeah, we buy dried beef in cans. Figgeh that! All yuh have to do is to knock a steer on the head, leave him hang for a coupla days – dried beef. Ain'tcha hungry?'

Sad laughed and shoved back from the table.

'What about that female person?' asked Elastic. 'Is she still down in Cinco? Yeah? She ain't goin' to git far, is she? Who do you suppose killed Charley Tolman? Wasn't it funny about findin' the body of Lobo Wolf in that coffin? Pretty danged swell fer an Injun, eh? I heard 'em say somethin' about Frank Welden's place burnin' down. Did, eh? Well, I've allus said that Cinco City would come into her own, if yuh give her time. Pima allus kicked about this place bein' too dead to squeak. I hope he's satisfied.'

'I suppose he is – in a way,' laughed Sad. 'Did you or Pima ever get any letters from John Cleland?'

'I got one from him oncet.'

239

'Still got it?'

'No-o-o. I never kept it. Somebody wrote it fer him on one of them there type machines.'

'Would you know the signature, if yuh saw it?'

'Nope. He wasn't much of a writer.'

'I guess he wasn't.'

'None of us old-timers write much.' Sad realized that there was nothing to learn from Elastic Jones; so they thanked him for the breakfast and rode away.

'Good luck to you in yore detectin',' laughed Elastic. 'You've shore got a fruitful field for yore labors, as the preacher said to himself.'

'Well, that didn't help much,' said Sad, as they rode back to Cinco City. 'They've spread the news that I'm a detective, it seems. That's bad. It marks us as Exhibit A. It seems to me that Tom Hawker was lookin' for information – and got it. All right, Mr. Hawker – turn yore wolf loose and we'll try and harvest his hide.'

'It seems to me we ought to have a showdown with Mr. Welden,' said Swede. 'You've got the goods on him.'

'In a way we have; but he ain't to blame for all this deviltry. He's only one bad boy in this school, and if we spank him too quick, it might ruin the next class. There's plenty

240

action comin' – don't worry.'

Frank Welden paid to send Tolman's body back to his old home in Detroit, but Lobo Wolf was laid to rest in the little Cinco cemetery that afternoon. The people around the town threw money into a hat to pay for the cheap casket. The plot was free and the minister kindly donated his services. There were no mourners. Tom Hawker, Pete Hawker, and Mike Joe were there. Mike Joe sat on the little fence, humped up in a dirty *serape*, although the sun was blistering hot. He munched peanuts, while the men shovelled dirt in on top of the remains of his bunkie. Sad and Swede went to the funeral and helped shovel dirt.

When they went back to the hotel, they found Andy Tolliver sitting in a buckboard in front of the hotel, talking with Melancholy.

'Miss Nolan is goin' out to the Circle Dot for a little visit,' said Andy. 'Aunt Minnie came in with me. She'd been askin' about Miss Nolan, and she kinda thought it was a shame she wasn't invited out to see folks. They're in the hotel now.'

'That's fine,' said Sad. He wanted Clare out of town, and he knew she would be safe at the Circle Dot.

A few minutes later, Clare and Mrs. Haskell came out. Mrs. Haskell, or Aunt Minnie, as

241

she was generally known, was a short, chubby little woman, past middle age, with a round face and big glasses. Clare introduced her to Sad and Swede, and she beamed upon them in a motherly way.

'I'm takin' Miss Nolan out for a few days,' she said breathlessly. 'I need company and so does she. There's so many things happenin' around this town that it ain't a fit place for a young lady. I was tellin' Bill – that's Mr. Haskell – that I thought it was a shame to let this lady stay at such a place as this hotel. I wouldn't. Nosiree! Not Minnie Haskell. Andy, are yuh ready to start back? Git in, Miss Nolan. Seat's kinda narrer, but we don't mind settin' familiar.

'Come out and see us, boys. Can't remember yore names, but names don't matter at the Circle Dot. Just step off yore broncs and you're at home. Andy, you've got the left line in yore right hand. Pretty wimmin always did have a queer effect on you. Oh, yuh needn't scrooge over too far, Mr. Tolliver.'

Aunt Minnie laughed breathlessly and grasped the side of the seat, when Andy swung the team sharply, and waved back at the three men.

'She's great,' laughed Melancholy. 'Yuh never get the blues around her. Allus the same. Mothers cowpunchers to death.

242

Doctors all of 'em, preaches the gospel when they need preachin' – and don't think she can't cuss yuh out. Mistreat an animal – whooee-e-e! Yessir, she's great.'

'Regular old-timer, eh?' laughed Sad.

'Y'betcha. Growed up with the hills. Yuh got Lobo planted all right?'

'Fit for a king.'

'I can beat yuh at fifteen-ball call-shot,' challenged Swede.

'You've done choosed my medicine,' grinned Melancholy, and they headed for the Cinco Saloon pool-table.

Sad sauntered into the hotel. There was no one in sight. Back of the little desk hung a board containing the doorkeys. Clare's key was there, and Sad quickly substituted his key for the one to her room, and put her key in his pocket. There would be a passenger train in from the west about eight o'clock, and Sad figured that Harold Welden would be on that train.

Things were quiet around town that evening, and when Sad heard the train whistle for Cinco City, he went up to Clare's room, let himself in quietly, and locked the door.

He knew Welden was in his room, because of the light through the transom over the door. It was nearly thirty minutes after the arrival of the train before anyone came down

243

the hallway of the hotel. It was a man walking slowly, as though looking for a number.

Sad heard a sharp knock on Welden's door, and after a short period of silence, Welden's voice, asking who was there.

'This is Hal,' said the man in the hallway.

Sad heard the door creak open.

'What in the world are you doing here?' asked Frank Welden.

The door shut sharply and a valise thumped on the floor.

'Doing here?' queried a heavy voice. 'You wired me to come.'

'I wired you?'

'You certainly did. You said for me to come at once, as you needed advice. I sent you a reply, saying I was leaving at once. What's wrong with you?'

'Something must be wrong, Hal. I never sent you any wire, and I never had one from you.'

'That's dam' queer.'

'It certainly is queer.'

'What's all this about your house burning down? I asked a man where I could find your place, and he said –'

'Don't talk so loud. This old place is a sound-box. Somebody did burn my house.'

'Well, what's gone wrong, anyway? You're as nervous as an old lady. Sit down and let's talk this thing over.'

'We can't talk here. Mebbe we better take a walk.'

'Suit yourself. Is Clare Nolan here yet?'

'In the next room' – softly – 'but she's away now. I've got plenty to tell you. Perhaps it's just as well you did come, but I don't understand about that telegram. It may be a trick of some kind. We'll go out the rear door of this place. I'm afraid to go out on the street at night.'

'Afraid?' sneeringly. 'I thought you bossed this town.'

'Sh-h-h-h! These partitions are as thin as paper.'

'You need a shot of liquor, Frank. There's a bottle in my valise.'

'Bring it along.'

Sad heard them lock the door and go down the hallway to the rear. He let himself out, locked Clare's door and went down to the lobby, where he switched the keys again, when he left his key on the board. Sad realized that there was no chance to overhear any more; so he sat down in the lobby, waiting for them to come back.

In half an hour Swede came in and Sad told him about the meeting of the Welden brothers.

'Oh, that's who he was, eh?' grunted

245

Swede. 'I was down at the stable when Welden came in with another man. They took a horse and buggy.'

'Which way did they go?' asked Sad quickly.

'They turned to the right, as though headin' for Aztec Wells or the Circle C.'

'Welden saw you?'

'Shore.'

Sad grinned thoughtfully. 'Aztec Wells or Circle C, eh? Well, we might as well go to bed. No use tryin' to foller a buggy in the dark.'

'Where do yuh think they went?'

'*Quien sabe?*'

'They told the stableman they might want the rig all night, 'cause they had a long trip to make. Welden asked for a certain horse which can stand a long trip. Looks like Aztec Wells, eh?'

'If yuh figure on looks – yeah.'

Frank Welden was back on the job at ten o'clock the next morning. Sad found Hal Welden was registered at the hotel and was sleeping late. The stableman told Sad that Welden and his brother didn't get back to town till six o'clock that morning.

'Took a long trip, eh?' queried Sad.

'The horse didn't look fagged.'

Sad went over to the courthouse, where he

talked with the prosecuting attorney about the Cleland will. It was the first time the lawyer had seen the will, but he had heard a lot about it. He said Tolman had told him that the will was not genuine; that it had not been signed by Cleland.

'But I would record it if I were you,' he said. 'If it should happen to be destroyed, there would be no legal record left. I'm merely taking Tolman's word that the thing is not genuine; but I can say to you that it looks genuine to me, and from what you say, I'd surely go to the trouble of having it recorded.'

'It's just so darn genuine that there are men who would murder me to get it,' laughed Sad. 'Will you record it and keep it in yore safe?'

'Why, certainly.'

Sad felt better, with the will out of his hands. It was about noon when he met the sheriff at the restaurant.

'Did you see Welden?' asked Panamint. 'He was lookin' for yuh. Said his brother was here from Los Angeles, and that his brother is familiar with Cleland's writin'. He wants to see that will. Says his brother can tell at a glance if it's Cleland's writin'.' The sheriff grinned slowly. 'He never said a word about how his brother happened to come here. I wish you'd tell me why yuh sent that wire.'

'Just to get that brother out here. Didja ever hear that old sayin' which is somethin' like "Whom the gods would destroy they first make mad"?'

'Oh,' thoughtfully. 'Are yuh aimin' to destroy somebody?'

'That,' smiled Sad thinly, 'is on the laps of the gods, Panamint. I'm workin' on a theory, and the play has got to come up jist right or it won't work. There's two factions I've got cinched; two outfits facin' the penitentiary. But I've got to tie 'em too tight for a slip. I'll let you in on the deal when the time is ripe.'

'I'll be all set,' grimly. 'If you can unravel this situation, I'll shore take my hat off to you, tall feller. All I do is eat and sleep, waitin' for the next break to come.'

'It'll come. Yuh can't pyramid crimes. Any time yuh get a gang so desperate that they have to murder to save their skins – they're goners.'

'But suppose they get you first, Sontag?'

'That's the fly in the axle grease.'

Sad left the restaurant and went back to the hotel, where the proprietor handed him an envelope, addressed but not stamped.

'It was on the desk. I dunno who left it,' he said.

Sad tore it open and read:

248

DEAR SAD:
  Come out to Circle C this afternoon if possible.

                                        CLARE

Sad sat down, took out the letter he had purloined from the bank, and compared the writing in the note with the signature on the letter which had been signed by Clare. The C's in the signatures were entirely different. In fact, none of the three capital C's in the note was like the one in the Cleland signature, nor were the small letters alike.

There was no question in his mind that it was a decoy letter, and somewhere on the Circle C road was an ambush. Sad found Swede at the sheriff's office and they went to the livery stable for their horses.

Swede asked no questions until they were out of town, when Sad told him about the note. But they did not follow the road. Sad led the way in a wide circle through the hills, well away from the road, and they came in at the opposite side of the ranch without seeing anybody.

They found Andy Tolliver and Pecan Cassidy at the corral, and the two cowboys welcomed them with a grin.

'It's about time yuh came out,' laughed Andy. 'We was talkin' about yuh last night, and Aunt Minnie said she'd bet both of yuh would come out soon, as long as Miss Nolan was here. Yuh met her, didn't yuh?'

'Met her?' queried Sad blankly.

'Yeah – on the road. Her and Ward Bellew left here about fifteen minutes ago, headin' for Cinco City.'

'There was a letter for her,' said Pecan. 'I got it in town this mornin'.'

'There's Aunt Minnie on the porch – she'd know about it.'

Sad swung his horse around and galloped up to the porch, where Mrs. Haskell was waiting for him.

'Oh, you are Mr. Sontag, aren't you?' she asked.

'Yes, ma'am.'

'Did you come by the road?'

'No, ma'am; we came through the hills.'

'That's how yuh missed 'em. Miss Nolan got your note and –'

'My note?'

'Why, yes, the note you mailed her. Pecan brought –'

'Did you see that note, Mrs Haskell?'

'Clare read it to me. It said you had something important to talk with her about this afternoon and –'

But Sad waited no longer. He swung his horse around and spurred straight for the three men at the corral.

'Saddle quick, boys!' he yelled. 'There's hell to pay, but don't ask questions now!'

The two Circle C cowboys ran for the stable, while Aunt Minnie came down across the yard, trying to find out what was wrong.

'I never wrote her a note,' said Sad. 'It was a scheme to get her away from here. I got a note from her and I knew she didn't write it. They wanted to get both of us at the same time. Why didn't I warn her to look out for somethin' like that! I reckon I'm getting dumb.'

'There's rifles in the bunk-house!' yelled Andy from outside the stable door. 'Shells on the shelf over the table.'

They spurred over to the bunk-house and secured the rifles and ammunition. By that time the two cowboys were ready. They each took a rifle and a box of cartridges, spurring away behind Sad, as they stuffed shells into the loading-gates of their rifles.

'Watch for the team and buckboard!' warned Sad. 'They'll probably be off the road.'

CHAPTER XV

Sad realized that Clare and Bellew were at least fifteen minutes ahead, and that many things could happen in that length of time. Bellew would probably drive fast, making almost as much speed as a man on horseback over that twisting road.

Sad rode high in his stirrups, scanning the country, leaving his horse to pick his own way over the road, while at his flank rode Swede with Andy and Pecan fully fifty feet behind, whipping their slower mounts to a top speed.

They whirled around a short curve, where the road ran along the side of a brushy swale, and Sad saw the buckboard and team down along the brush. A touch on the reins and his horse bunched its feet in a sliding stop. The other riders lurched past, throwing showers of gravel. They could see the team tied to a willow snag, and on the ground beside the buckboard was the figure of a man.

Swede and the other two cowboys headed for the buckboard, but Sad spurred to higher ground. His keen eyes had caught the flash of color through an opening in the tangle of brush on the slope beyond. He could see better now, as the escaping riders angled toward a canyon to the left. They were at least four hundred yards away and going fast.

Because of the thick brush it was impossible to determine how many riders there were, or the colors of their horses. Sad swung up his rifle, quickly adjusted the cheap open sights. He did not realize that he was against the skyline from their position, nor that they had seen him, until a bullet, flying low, screamed off a rock a few feet below him.

Two of the riders were going in single file, and now they swung a little higher, trying to get around an outcropping of granite, both riders apparently humped low over their horses' necks. For a space of a few seconds they were broadside to Sad, and in those few seconds he had lined up the sights of his thirty-thirty rifle and squeezed the trigger. It was a long shot and a snap-shot. The rear horse whirled, pawing at the air, seemed to turn completely around on its hind legs, and went backward into the brush.

Sad spurred quickly down the hill toward the buckboard, while several misdirected bullets spattered around the hill above him. Swede and Pecan were running toward Sad, trying to locate the shooters, but Sad waved them back, as he came down the hill.

'Keep under cover!' he yelled. 'They're in

253

thick brush over there, and we ain't got much chance – yet.'

'That's Ward down there,' panted Pecan. 'He got hit over the head, but he's all right. Somebody bushed 'em – masked men. One of 'em popped him on the head with a rifle barrel. He was hog-tied and blindfolded. Says he only saw two men, and he didn't know where Miss Nolan went.'

Pecan was out of breath panting his information. Ward Bellew, who had driven the buckboard, was propped up against a wheel, nursing his head with both hands, but he tried to grin at Sad. He didn't have a clear recollection of what had happened, it seemed.

'Two men, I think,' he said painfully. 'There at the curve. They had the drop on me, and one held the team while the other came back on my side of the rig, coverin' me with a rifle. They both wore black masks. The man says to me to look over there, and I looked where he pointed. That's all I know, except that somethin' landed on my head.

'Dam' funny thing to happen, eh? There's another thing, too. Mebby I heard it before he hit me, it might have been afterwards, 'cause it was kinda like the things yuh hear when they give yuh chloroform. Yuh know what I mean? One of them little voices miles and miles away, but plenty plain. Well, it sounded like Miss Nolan's voice, miles and miles away, yellin' – "Chuck!" '

'Yellin' for Chuck, eh?' grunted Sad.

'Mebby I dreamed it, Sontag; but I'd swear it wasn't no dream.'

'Well, let's go gunnin' for them gents,' said Swede impatiently.

'Take it easy,' advised Sad. 'They're under cover now, and they'd shore smoke us up plenty. I dropped one horse. They can't stop to take the horse with 'em, and it ought to be pretty bad evidence against 'em, unless they're smart enough to cut off the brand and skin out other spots; so we wouldn't know the location of the real brand. I've known things like that to be done.'

'But they've got that girl with 'em,' protested Swede.

'Shore they have. And any long-range shootin' might hurt her. Yuh can't tell a woman from a man at four or five hundred yards. Can you take care of yourself, Ward?'

'I'm all right, except for a headache; go right ahead.'

They mounted their horses and headed through the swale, keeping down in the brush as much as possible, but gradually working toward the outcropping of granite. There was no more shooting. Finally Sad rode out of the brush and headed for the rocks. There were tracks of several horses in soft spots, but nothing else to be seen until he rode in above the rocks. Just below him, piled in close to the rocks, was the body of a sorrel horse, all four feet in the air. The cinch around the belly attested to the fact that they never stopped to remove the saddle.

The other three men joined him and they dismounted quickly, sliding down the hill beside the dead horse.

'Hello!' grunted Pecan. 'What's this?'

It was a man, lying half-buried in the brush just below the horse. Quickly they lifted him out to an open spot and placed him on his back.

It was Chuck Gavin, bruised and unconscious. The men looked silently at each other, as Sad knelt down beside Chuck, trying to find out how badly he was injured, while the other three squatted on their heels and rolled smokes. As far as Sad could determine, no bones were broken. His hands and face had been cut in several places.

'I knowed that sorrel as soon as I seen him,' said Andy. 'It's Chuck's saddle animal.'

Sad walked down in the brush a few feet away, where he picked up a piece of white cloth about two feet square. It was wrinkled, torn in one place, and in the middle of it was a bloodstain several inches across. It was a piece of an old flour sack.

'Mask, eh?' grunted Andy.

'No eye-holes,' said Sad, thoughtfully studying Chuck Gavin.

'Kinda funny – leavin' him thataway,' said Pecan.

'Must have been in a hurry,' said Andy. 'Mebby they was afraid to take a chance on stoppin'.'

'That's probably it,' agreed Swede.

'And,' observed Pecan dryly, 'this is shore goin' to make that J Bar 44 outfit hard to catch.'

'We'll make somebody hard to catch,' replied Sad. 'Let's carry him back to the rig.'

They carried Chuck over to the horses, where they sprawled him across a saddle and took him back to the buckboard. Ward Bellew felt too miserable to ask questions; so they sent him back to the ranch on Pecan's horse, while Pecan drove the team to Cinco City. They stopped in front of the sheriff's office and carried Chuck inside, where Sad explained what had happened, before sending for the doctor.

Quite a crowd gathered around, but Sad had warned the boys to keep still about what had happened. Swede told them that Chuck had been thrown from his horse, but none of them seemed to believe that story. Panamint closed the door against the crowd, and only he and Sad stayed with the doctor.

'Slight concussion,' said the doctor. 'I don't think it is dangerous. He must have struck something pretty hard. How did it happen?'

Sad told him, and the doctor was properly amazed.

'I'm goin' to lock him up,' decided the sheriff. 'You can take care of him here in the jail, Doc.'

'I'd lock him up,' agreed Sad. 'At least he's better off there until we know more about things. The people might get nasty over this thing, and we don't want any lynch lawyers holdin' court around here.'

'Our next move is to get out to the J Bar 44,' said the sheriff grimly.

But Sad shook his head quickly.

'Why not?' snorted Panamint wonderingly.

'Because it'll take more brains than brawn to clear this deal. If they wanted to kill Miss Nolan, they'd never have stolen her. She's all right for a while. Rushin' out there and startin' trouble won't get us any place. Let me work out a little scheme, will yuh?'

'Well, I suppose I will,' helplessly. 'You seem to be the only one who has any ideas a-tall; so go ahead and keep thinkin'.'

The sheriff forgot to swear the doctor to secrecy over what had happened, and the crowd got most of the story from him. Sad realized that the country would be aroused and that the sheriff would have a difficult time in keeping his prisoner. Chuck Gavin was still unconscious, unable to make any kind of an explanation.

'Why not send word to the J Bar 44?' asked Sad. 'Tell Bat Gavin what happened. We don't want this boy lynched.'

Panamint's jaw sagged at the suggestion.

'Send for Bat Gavin? Are you plumb loco, Sontag?'

'Not yet; it was merely a suggestion.'

'Good – hell! And why send for Bat Gavin?'

'To help protect Chuck.'

'Help who – me? I ort to go out there and arrest the whole outfit.'

Sad grinned slowly. 'I reckon I'll go and tell 'em about it.'

'They don't need to be told – they know it already.'

'Just the same, I'm goin' out there.'

'My gosh, yo're stubborn as a mule and as crazy as a shepherd. Ain't yuh got a lick of sense?'

'That remains to be seen,' said Sad, as he walked out.

'Yo're a dam' fool!' yelled Panamint.

'Yeah, and I've got plenty company around here,' retorted Sad, as he mounted his horse and rode swiftly out of town.

Sad had let the sheriff read the decoy note, asking him to come out to the Circle C. Ranch.

'The darn fool is goin' out there,' wailed the sheriff from the office door. 'They try to bushwhack him with a fake note, and now he deliberately goes out to talk with 'em. If he gets back alive, he's a wonder.'

But Sad was not afraid of being bushwhacked this time. He did not meet anyone on the road and the first man he saw at the J Bar 44 Ranch was Dick Ellers, Chuck's cousin. Ellers looked him over rather curiously when Sad asked to see Bat Gavin.

'He's up at the house,' said Ellers shortly, and turned back to the stable.

Sad rode up to the porch and dismounted as Bat Gavin came out.

The old man nodded shortly.

'Can yuh spare a few minutes?' asked Sad.

'All yuh need. What's gone wrong now?'

Sad motioned to a chair.

'Set down, Gavin; and set on yore gun hand. I've got a tale to tell.'

Wonderingly the owner of the J Bar 44 sat down and listened, while Sad told him what had happened on the road to the Circle C. Several times the hard-faced old cattleman started to interrupt, but changed his mind.

He was staring blankly into space when Sad finished.

'That's a queer story, Sontag,' he said slowly. 'Dam' queer. I wonder what's the answer. Yuh say he ain't hurt bad?'

'Bad enough.'

'And he's in jail, eh?'

'Don't blame anybody for that.'

'I'm not. It looks bad for Chuck. A lot of these dam' fools –' he stopped and clenched his jaws tightly. 'They'd like to get the Gavin family.'

Suddenly he struck the arm of his chair with a horny fist.

'By gosh, I'll take my men and wreck that jail! Let 'em try to stop us. I'll take that boy out of that town and –'

'That wouldn't prove anythin',' said Sad mildly. 'Yuh don't want him out, with a charge like that hangin' over him, Gavin.'

The old man relaxed slowly, shaking his head. 'No. I reckon yo're right. But we can't let them lynch him. That jail won't keep 'em out. The sheriff is on the square, but he won't sacrifice his own neck to save a prisoner. What's to be done?'

'Come to town after dark. Bring all yore men and come in behind the jail. I'll see that the sheriff is lookin' for yuh. They won't do anythin' until after dark, anyway – if they do

261

then. I'm hopin' they don't. But if they do, it may take force to make 'em see things in the right light.'

'The rest of my men will be here at supper-time; and we'll be in Cinco before seven o'clock, Sontag.'

Gavin got to his feet and held out his hand to Sad.

'They tell me yo're a cattle detective. Anyway, that's the report the boys got. But no matter who yuh are, I want to thank yuh for this, and if there's any way we can help yuh put the deadwood where it belongs, all you've got to do is ask us. We'd shore like to see things put straight. For many years we've been known as the tough Gavins. They say we're cattle rustlers, gunmen, and everythin' else. If somebody pulls off a rough job out here – the J Bar 44 gets the blame. They even hint that we killed John Cleland. If he'd stayed out here, one of us would, prob'ly; but none of us would go out of our way to plug the old geezer. He killed my brother. I can't swear it wasn't an even break, but I don't believe it was. But that don't matter.

'With the reputation we've got, it'll go hard with Chuck, even in a court of law. It wouldn't be hard to get a jury to convict him. From what you say, it shore looks mighty bad. Chuck's wild as a young hawk, but as wild as he is, he'd never harm a woman. A Gavin never harmed a woman.'

Sad smiled as they shook hands.

'I hope he don't get worse than a headache, Gavin. So-long.'

Sad rode back to Cinco City and stabled his horse. He found Swede at the hotel nervously waiting his return.

'They said yuh went out to the Gavin place,' he said. 'Panamint shore is all sweaty over it. What happened, anyway?'

'Nothin'. Anything new here?'

'Not a thing. Mike Joe was in from the Tomahawk and somebody bought him a bottle of liquor. He thought he was Sittin' Bull when he rode home, emittin' plenty war-whoops.'

'Chuck woke up yet?'

'Yeah, he woke up jist after you left. He's all right. The sheriff told him what he was up against, and he refused to talk at all.'

'That's the best thing for him to do.'

'I found out another thing – Harold Welden went away on a train this mornin'.'

'He did, eh? Which way, do yuh know?'

'West.'

Sad sprawled in his chair and drew his sombrero down over his eyes.

'Went away, eh?'

'It don't spoil anythin' for yuh, does it?'

asked Swede anxiously.

'*Quien sabe?* Time will tell. So he went away. Hm-m-m-m-m.'

The town was quiet until after supper, when the cowboys began drifting in. All the men from the JHC came in, even to Elastic Jones, who went up to the hotel to visit with Pima Simpson. They came from the Circle Dot, bringing Ward Bellew, with his head swathed in bandages. Uncle Billy Haskell came along, anxious for more news of Clare Nolan. Pete Hawker came in and was around town awhile, but went back to tell the news.

Sad had a long talk with Panamint and Melancholy about the J Bar 44 outfit. Panamint was doubtful over the scheme. He contended that there would be a big scrap in town as soon as the rest of the men heard that the Gavins were in.

'Keep 'em out of town, until the trouble starts,' suggested Sad.

'You stay here and handle it.'

'I'll be pretty busy.'

'Passin' the buck to me, eh? Well, all right.'

Sad wanted to keep an eye on Frank Welden, and he saw the banker go to the hotel just after dark. Sad had left his horse at the hitch-rack near the sheriff's office, and when he saw Welden go into the hotel, he instructed

Swede to watch the front of the hotel while he watched the rear. If Welden came out the front, Swede was to notify Sad at once.

But Frank Welden did not come out the front. It was dark when he came down the rear steps of the hotel, crossed the litter of stuff in the back yard, and went out toward where his house had stood. Sad trailed as closely as he dared, and in the dim light he saw Welden meet a man with two horses and they rode away together, circling the town to the road, which might take them out to the JHC, the J Bar 44, or to the Tomahawk. Sad went back, told Swede to stay with the sheriff, and followed them.

Sad had a feeling that the man with Welden was Pete Hawker, who had been in town, but went away again.

There was no moon, but the stars were bright. Sad rode at a moderate pace. He did not think they would expect to be followed by anyone from town; so he was not careful, feeling that they would ride to the ranch as quickly as possible. He was playing a hunch, but when he reached the Tomahawk, he wondered if his intuition had not been all wrong. Not a light was showing in the old ranch-house.

He dismounted at a distance and tied his horse behind some brush near the fence.

Crawling through the fence, he approached the house from the rear, praying that the Tomahawk did not own a barking dog. He circled some outbuildings and reached the corral. Here he found two saddled horses tied to the fence. On the other side of the corral he found a horse and buggy. It was too dark to tell much about this outfit, but, after feeling the animal over, he decided that it had not been driven for several hours, as its coat was perfectly dry.

Circling back the way he came, he examined the saddled horses, speaking softly to them. They were wet from fast traveling, and Sad grinned widely to himself. His hunch had been vindicated. The next thing to do was to find out what was going on in the house. The windows were evidently blanketed to prevent any lights showing. He sneaked around the house and came in close to the window, but was unable to hear anything.

He tried the window on the opposite side with like results, and finally went down to the corral near the buggy, wondering what to do next. He was positive there were people in the house, but just who, and what they were doing, he could only make a guess. He could see the house plainly in the starlight. Suddenly he crouched down beside the fence. The figure of a man was stealing along the side of the house toward the window. Sad could see him plainly. He stood at the window for a minute or two, stole quietly back and went around the rear of the house.

'Two of us, eh?' muttered Sad. 'This looks interesting. Who is that jigger, and what is he doin' here, I wonder?'

Sad hunched there on his heels, wondering what it was all about, and he was about to go on an investigating tour, when the front door suddenly opened, letting out a flood of light. Figures came out on the porch. A man laughed softly. Now there were two people coming down toward Sad, while the rest stayed on the porch. Sad hunched motionless, as he watched the two dark forms come down across the yard, heading for the buggy.

Neither of them spoke. They were at the buggy now, and a faint odor of perfume was wafted to Sad's nostrils. The horse shifted uneasily and a man's voice spoke soothingly.

Suddenly the stillness was shattered by the heavy report of a gun, and a man screamed. It was up there by the front porch. There were more reports; revolver shots, one – two – three, spaced evenly.

The man at the buggy went running toward the house, questioning as he ran.

Sad acted quickly. He ran round to the buggy, gun in hand.

'Clare!' he called sharply. 'Clare, is that you?'

No answer, except a movement of the person. He reached over the side of the seat. A woman's dress, ropes! Quickly he unfastened the tie-rope, sprang into the seat, and whirled the horse around.

Sad knew the road. Just ahead was the big gate, sagging open, and he sent that horse at a running gallop, barely missing the right-hand post as he swung out through and headed toward Cinco City. He heard a yell from the house, and thought he heard the word 'runaway,' but he wasn't sure. The top of the buggy was down, but behind him was only a cloud of dust; so he was unable to see what was happening back there at the Tomahawk.

But Sad knew there was no chance for him to outrun saddle-horses. The road was heavy, much of it upgrade, and after the first half-mile, the buggy horse would be played out. He had no idea what all the shooting was about, but he was sure that at least two riders would be following him quickly; so he checked his horse, swung off the road through a swale, and went twisting and lurching down through the brush, where the buggy threatened to upset at any moment.

A hundred yards off the road, he stopped the horse behind some brush, sprang out and

268

tied the animal quickly. He scratched a match and looked at his companion of the wild ride. It was Clare, gagged and blindfolded. Quickly he stripped the cloth from her face, and her frightened eyes blinked at the match. He cut the ropes in the darkness.

'Are yuh all right, Clare?' he asked. 'Yuh ain't hurt none?'

'Sad?' she whispered hoarsely.

'That's me. Yo're all right now. Stay right here, and I'll be back in a few minutes. We've got to have my horse.'

'I'm all right,' she whispered.

Sad ran back through the brush in time to see two horsemen galloping swiftly along the road to Cinco City. They swung past the top of the swale and kept on going. Sad ran down the road, going straight back to the ranch-house. The front door was still open, but there was no one in sight. Gun in hand he went cautiously along the side of the house, halted for a moment at the corner of the porch, and then went to the lighted doorway.

The only occupant of the room was the body of a man, stretched out in the middle of the floor. Sad looked him over, but stepped out quickly.

It was Frank Welden, the Cinco City banker – dead.

Sad stopped on the porch. He could see

the glow of a light through the open stable door; so he went down there as silent as an Indian, in spite of his high-heeled boots and spurs. A man was in one of the stalls, saddling by the light of an old lantern. He backed the animal out and started to lead it outside, but stopped short, with Sad's six-shooter pressing against the lower button of his vest.

'Yore name's Harold Welden, ain't it?' asked Sad.

'That is mum-my name,' stammered Welden nervously.

'Turn around, Welden.'

The lawyer obeyed, and Sad relieved him of an automatic pistol.

'This is ridiculous,' growled Welden. 'Why hold me up?'

'That is somethin' for the judge to decide. Keep yore hands up and get on that horse. No time to answer questions now.'

'You don't need to rope me on.'

'Yo're the only one who knows that, Welden.'

A few minutes later, they came from the stable, Sad leading the horse, while Harold Welden, well roped, wondered what would happen to him. He looked at the open door of the ranch-house, but said nothing. They circled the fence to where Sad had left his horse, and from there they rode back through the brush to where Sad had left Clare in the buggy. Sad felt sure that the two men who had pursued him would be coming back soon, trying to find where the vehicle had left the road.

Sad called softly to Clare as they rode up, and she answered him.

'Got an old friend of yours, Clare – Harold Welden, Esquire.'

'I recognized his voice,' she said.

'When was that?'

'Before you came. They were all masked. I had my choice of leaving the country – or never leaving it. They were taking me to a railroad and giving me a ticket back to Los Angeles, and they made me sign a paper which said I was an impostor – that I never knew John Cleland. They threatened –'

'I suppose our lawyer friend has the paper,' laughed Sad. 'A lot of good it'll do him. Frank Welden is down at the ranch-house, shot full of holes, and as dead as a gimlet.

'I kinda figured on this, yuh see. Our lawyer friend here pulled out on a mornin' train from Cinco, and went to Tejunga, where he hired a rig and drove back here. Any comments to make, Welden?'

'Not to you,' hoarsely.

'No use wastin' breath, then,' laughed Sad.

'Clare, we'll have to ride my horse double, if yo're able to ride.'

'Oh, I haven't been hurt.'

'Fine. Yuh can tell me the rest of it on the way to town. We've got to keep off the road or we may never get there. Now, Welden, if we meet anybody and you let out a single yip – I'll fill yuh full of lead.'

'But I haven't done anything,' protested Welden.

'Then you'll die innocent; but I'll never believe it.'

CHAPTER XVI

In the meantime things were not going so well in Cinco City. Swede recognized the signs and prayed for Sad to come back. The Cinco City Saloon was full of men drinking and arguing, and Swede knew they were building up a case against Chuck Gavin. Ted Bell was the big agitator.

Panamint was worried, as was Melancholy. The jail was not built to withstand an assault, and Panamint realized that in case of an assault, someone was sure to get hurt. The sheriff of Cinco was not going to relinquish his prisoner without an argument.

Melancholy kept watch for the J Bar 44 outfit, and notified the sheriff as soon as Gavin and his men were behind the jail. Panamint went out and had a talk with old Bat Gavin.

'Let 'em come,' growled Gavin. 'We'll back up the law for yuh.'

'And start a new graveyard. We don't want any killin', Bat.'

'Then see that they leave Chuck alone.'

'Ain't I tryin' to do that? If Sontag had kept his long nose out of this, we'd be all right.'

'The lynchin' would be over and everybody satisfied, eh?'

'We don't want no war.'

No one saw the figure crouched at a corner of the jail, listening to the conversation. He edged back and went swiftly across the street to the Cinco Saloon.

'What charge have yuh got against Chuck?' demanded his father.

'Charge?' queried the sheriff blankly. 'Why, I – I'll –'

Bat Gavin came in closer to the sheriff.

'Panamint, you ain't even arrested that boy. There's no charge against him.'

The sheriff was silent, knowing Bat Gavin was right. They had merely locked Chuck in the jail.

273

'Yuh can't hold him,' said Bat Gavin. 'There's no charge against him and yuh never arrested him. Now, dam' yuh, open that jail and let him out.'

Panamint's arms lifted slightly as he felt the muzzle of Bat Gavin's gun against his chest. He started to protest, to argue; but the muzzle was eloquent.

'Yore keys,' said Gavin coldly. 'Either yuh give 'em to me, or I take 'em.'

'In my pants pocket,' growled Panamint, and swore bitterly as one of the men reached in his pocket and took them out.

'Go in the back door and bring him out,' said Bat Gavin.

'You'll pay for this, Bat,' wailed the sheriff. 'Yuh can't do things like that.'

'Can't I – you watch. You'll keep no son of mine in jail, where they can take him out and lynch him – not unless there's a charge against him. You won't make it hot for me, Panamint, 'cause it's yore mistake, not mine. The law will back me in this.'

They were grouped at the rear door as two of the boys came out with Chuck.

'Are yuh all right, Chuck?' asked his father.

'Shore, Dad.'

'Let's go, boys.'

But Chuck's escape had been effected just too late. They turned from the rear door of the jail to face several rifles, while more men came quietly around the other corner of the jail. The J Bar 44 was surrounded, outnumbered.

'Collect their guns,' ordered Ted Bell. 'Bring plenty ropes, and let's get this business over with.'

'What's your big idea, Bell?' asked Panamint.

'That's none of yore damned business, and if you don't keep yore mouth shut, you'll be tied with the rest. We've got yore deputy cinched; so set still and keep yore mouth shut.'

'Better think it over,' advised the sheriff. 'There's a law against yuh takin' this in yore own hands. I can send every dam' one of yuh to the pen.'

'Where'd yuh find a jury to convict us?' laughed Bell.

'What'll we do with all these guns?' asked Mose Heilman.

'Hide 'em where they won't find 'em for a while. Lock 'em in the jail, that's a good place.'

'How about lockin' this whole dam' J Bar 44 outfit in there until this is over?' asked Larry Delago.

'Not much!' snapped Ted. 'I want 'em at the trial.'

'Where's that dam' detective Sontag and his pardner?' asked Heilman.

'You'll find out,' growled the sheriff.

'Is that so?' sneered Bell. 'If he shows up, we'll take him, too. All right, boys – get 'em all roped. Fine. C'mon over to the saloon, and we'll try this woman-stealer. We'll show Cinco City what law is made for.'

'You boys from the Circle Dot,' said the sheriff, 'won't stand for anything like this.'

'He stole that girl,' said Ward Bellew. 'Him and his outfit almost killed me, didn't they? What's a man got to do around here in order to be punished, anyway?'

'You recognized Chuck Gavin?'

'I heard that girl call his name.'

'What's the use of arguin'?' said Bell impatiently. 'He's as guilty as hell, and he knows it. He'll have a chance to make his talk over in the saloon. Mebby we'll cool off this Gavin outfit for a while.'

'You'll pay for it, Bell,' warned Bat Gavin. 'Arizona won't be big enough to hold me and you after tonight.'

'Don't brag, you old fool; there may not be any other night for you. This is the showdown we've been headin' to for a long time, and the JHC is on top.'

Swede saw them going toward the Cinco City Saloon. He knew what had happened;

276

saw them capture Melancholy in front of the saloon, but he didn't know what such a move meant. Swede was helpless against such numbers, and he wondered where Sad was. Tom Hawker and his outfit were not in town, and Swede wondered if Sad was out at the Tomahawk. Swede was mad. Hungering for action, he was obliged to steer clear of the crowd, waiting for Sad to show up, or for something else to happen.

He saw a man come from the crowded saloon and go to the hitch-rack. It was Uncle Billy Haskell getting ready to mount his horse, when Swede came up to him.

'The whole thing is wrong,' he declared. 'I'm goin' home and keep out of it. They're goin' to lynch Chuck Gavin just as sure as hell. They're all drunk, and I won't be no party to such a thing as that. And you better keep out of sight, Harrigan. They're lookin' for you and Sontag.'

'I'm lookin' for him, too,' sighed Swede.

'They're tryin' to make Chuck tell where that girl is, but he can't or won't tell anythin', except that he don't know a thing. He's tryin' to make 'em believe he rode into that holdup when they stole the girl, and they took him along with her, until somebody killed his horse. He don't know what happened after that, he says.'

'Won't yore men drop the job?'

'Sober – yes.'

'See if yuh can't get some of 'em out here. If we had a couple more men, we could clean up that bunch.'

'I'm afraid I can't get 'em out.'

'Pardner, yuh can't afford to be afraid when a man's life is at stake. Two more is all we need. Them sidewinders from the JHC will head for the brush if the goin' gets tough.'

'You seem to think Chuck is innocent.'

'If he ain't, we've got law, ain't we?' Swede replied hotly. 'They'll not hang that kid tonight, even if I have to stand out here in the street and pot-shoot at every dam' man that shows his head. I mean it, Haskell. Now you go and hammer some sense into yore drunken punchers.'

'I'll try it, but it won't work. They're pullin' off a trial in there, and I can't get at 'em, without everybody seein' me.'

Two men were coming across the street from the hotel, one going slowly. They were Elastic Jones and Pima Simpson. Old Pima was out at last, trembly but game, his arm in a sling. Swede stopped them and both men recognized him.

'Goin' to the party,' said Pima. 'No dam' doctor can stop me now.'

Quickly Swede explained what was going

278

on, and Pima laughed delightedly.

'I'd git off m' dyin' bed to see 'em lynch a Gavin.'

'Even if he wasn't guilty?' asked Swede.

'Hell! He'd be guilty enough.'

'Yuh danged right,' agreed Elastic, and Swede groaned. No help from that quarter.

A rider came pounding in and fairly fell off his horse at the hitch-rack. Swede thought for a moment that it was Sad, but in the salon lights he saw it was Tom Hawker. He had not even stopped to tie his horse, which went across the street, reins dragging. Hawker stopped just outside the doorway, and it seemed to Swede that he was looking back. Slowly he stepped inside.

Two more riders were coming at a gallop. At least there were two horses, but one carried a double burden. It was Sad, Clare, and Harold Welden.

'Who the hell is this?' grunted Elastic as Sad dismounted in the street and lifted Clare to the ground.

'Yo're just in time,' said Swede quickly. 'The JHC outfit captured the sheriff's office and the J Bar 44, and they're goin' to hang Chuck Gavin.'

'That so?' panted Sad. 'Did Tom Hawker come here?'

'About a minute ago.'

'I thought so. Hello, Haskell; we'll need you. Elastic, are yuh with us or against us?'

'Well, hell,' muttered Elastic. 'I want to be on the right side – me and Pima.'

'I'm ag'in them Gavins,' declared Pima.

'All right; you stay here with the horses and see that the man on that horse don't try to get away.'

'All right,' said Pima.

Sad's order had rather taken his breath away, and he didn't know what to say. Somehow he had faith in this lanky cowboy, and there was a chance that Sad was favoring the JHC.

'Stay here, Clare,' ordered Sad. 'Don't come near that salon, 'cause somethin' is liable to happen. C'mon, boys.'

With Sad in the lead, the four men walked straight into the salon. Chuck Gavin was backed against the bar, arms tied behind him, a rope around his neck. The three men from the JHC were close together in front of him, and Ward Bellew was telling them what had happened when Clare was kidnaped. Tom Hawker was standing near the door, and it was evident that he hadn't talked with anyone since his arrival.

The sheriff, Melancholy, and the boys from the J Bar 44 were grouped together against the opposite wall, and Andy Tolliver sat on a card-table, covering them with a rifle. Sad took this all in at a glance. Ward quit in the middle of a sentence and all eyes turned toward Sad, Swede, William Haskell, and Elastic Jones. They stopped short of the bar, and Sad smiled pleasantly around at the crowd.

'You can untie Chuck Gavin,' he said slowly. 'Yuh see, I've found Miss Nolan, and she says Chuck had no hand in that trouble.'

Chuck straightened up quickly. No one spoke, until Tom Hawker's voice broke the silence, with –

'Look out, Ted! Somebody killed Frank, and –'

Sock! Swede had turned and, when Tom Hawker started to speak, his right fist caught Hawker's chin in a looping uppercut, breaking his sentence off midway, and almost taking Hawker's jaw along with it. Mr. Hawker went down in a heap.

Still no one made any move. They looked at the crumpled figure on the floor, and at Swede, still hunched forward, opening and shutting his right hand, which had been numbed by the blow. Few men in the room knew what it was all about; few had heard what Hawker yelled at Ted Bell.

But Ted Bell heard, and he knew what it all meant. For an instant the blood seemed to drain from his face and his eyes flashed sideways, as though seeking a chance of escape. Bell was neither a coward nor a fool. He thought quickly, grasping at a straw. It was a slim chance – but a chance.

'All right,' he said, his voice strained and unnatural. 'If the girl says Gavin is innocent, we'll turn him loose. I'm willin' to admit I was wrong. Take the ropes off, boys. Everythin' is all right and I'm glad we got word in time. Take off the ropes and I'll buy a drink.'

Bell laughed shortly, shaking his nerves together quickly, and started toward the bar, but Sad's voice snapped like a whip.

'Just a moment, Bell!'

Ted Bell stopped short, whirling to face Sad Sontag. He was cornered, and he knew he was cornered. He could see it in the masklike face, the hard gray eyes of the tall puncher, who was swaying easily on his feet. Bell licked his lips and his face turned gray in the yellow light of the lamps. There were many other faces, but they were blurred. All he could see was that long face, yellow in the lamplight, and the ice-cold eyes. There was no compromise. Bell tried to steel his nerves, but it was no use. Sad was talking, and his voice had the hard metallic grate of a cheap phonograph.

'I've got yuh where the hair is short, Bell;

too short to save yuh from a rope. For two years you've been weavin' the rope that will snap yore neck. Harold Welden told me the whole scheme tonight. He's a yeller quitter, and a quitter always talks to save his own skin. I know all about the killin' of Cleland, the forged mortgage on the JHC, the stealin' of cattle by the Tomahawk.

'I know who hired Lobo Wolf to steal that will from Miss Nolan, and I know who killed Lobo Wolf. You and yore gang tried to ambush me, but I fooled yuh. Yuh kidnaped Miss Nolan, and when Chuck rode in on the holdup, yuh stuck him up and took him along. I know who held up that train, stole the money and the body and cut the train in two. I know all these things, and I've got yuh, Bell, you dirty murderer!'

Bell did not move. His jaw sagged a little. Down in his quaking heart he knew this man would kill him if he made a move. He wanted to lift his hands and cry quits, but what was the use? Gun or rope, where was the difference, in the end?

Larry Delago and Mose Heilman shifted uneasily, as though trying to get into a better position, but Andy Tolliver had already shifted his rifle to cover them both. They were helpless, staring wide-eyed at Sontag, who had already read their death-warrant.

Suddenly a man swore softly. The sheriff, deputy, and men from the J Bar 44 began moving along the wall, as though to get out of range of that doorway.

Ted Bell's eyes shifted from Sontag to whatever was in that doorway. Sad did not dare to turn his head.

It was Mike Joe, the Indian, naked to the waist, his face and body a smear of blood from a wound high up on his left shoulder. There was another purple hole in his chest lower down, but it wasn't bleeding – not outside. In his two hands was a double-barreled shotgun, both hammers at full-cock, the first two fingers of his grimy right hand locked around the triggers; the gun held waist-high, pointing at Ted Bell.

And deep in his skinny throat he was chanting a meaningless 'Hyah, hyah, hyah, hyah, hyah, hyah,' but the mummy-like features remained stolid. There was no use trying to stop him. Even a bullet would not prevent him from jerking the triggers.

'I come to kill,' he said chokingly. 'Tolman I kill before – tonight I kill Welden. Now I kill Bell, because he help kill Lobo Wolf. Mike Joe die pretty quick now, but he not die alone.'

Sad stepped aside. No one made any move to stop Mike Joe, whose beady eyes were

284

strained, unnatural, like the eyes of an animal.

'Mike Joe not afraid,' he said weakly. 'Nobody hurt Mike Joe. I fool everybody; now I kill –'

But Elastic Jones didn't relish the idea of Mike Joe using that shotgun on anybody, so he ducked low and flung himself at Joe's skinny legs. At the same instant Ted Bell's right hand streaked for his gun, but Sad had been looking for this. The two loads of buckshot tore through the ceiling, drowning the report of Sad's heavy revolver, and Ted Bell shocked in the middle of his draw, jerked back, dropping his gun, and went down heavily.

'If either of you jiggers make a move, I'll hang yuh both on the same bullet!' yelled Andy Tolliver.

But Larry Delago and Mose Heilman made no move, while the sheriff stepped over and took away their guns. Bell was cursing impotently over a smashed shoulder, and Elastic was sitting on Mike Joe. The room was in an uproar. Someone cut Chuck Gavin loose. He stood there bewildered until Sad said to him, 'She's out there in the street; kinda anxious, I reckon.'

Chuck nodded and stumbled out, the rope still trailing from his neck.

'Don't let that dam' Injun git that shotgun,'

warned Panamint. 'He ain't dead.'

'He shore won't,' replied Elastic, with both feet on the weapon.

Larry Delago and Mose Heilman were backed against the wall, while Swede and Melancholy roped them tightly. Other men were roping Hawker, who was slowly recovering from Swede's punch on his jaw.

Sad stepped over to Delago and Heilman ignoring Ted Bell, who was in a chair now, his face as white as woodashes.

'Either of you boys care to talk?' asked Sad.

'What's it worth to us?' asked Delago quickly.

'You'll find out at the trial – I'm makin' no promises. But yo're cinched; so yuh might as well talk. Welden was yaller.'

'I told Ted he was,' said Delago. 'Frank was yellow, too. But we got into the deal and couldn't get out. Ted and Frank planned to steal the JHC. Frank framed a fake mortgage. That was before the old man was killed. Hal Welden was in on the deal, and when the old man wanted to make out a will, Hal knew it would queer the deal; so he got drunk and shot him. He didn't know the old man might write one before he died.

'Hal kept us informed on when the body

would come, and Tolman framed the idea of us stealin' the body to keep her from provin' anythin'. Tolman was in on the deal, too, yuh know.'

'Was the JHC rich enough for all of yuh to have a finger in the pie?' asked Sad.

Delago licked his lips, tried to grin, but changed his mind.

'Go and look at the foundation of that JHC ranch-house. Cleland didn't know ore – but Frank Welden did. That ranch-house sets on top of a million-dollar gold mine.'

'You better shut up,' said Heilman hoarsely. 'No use runnin' our necks into a rope.'

'What about this Injun?' asked Elastic. 'Do I set on him all night?'

They propped Mike Joe up against the wall. The doctor was busy with Ted Bell, and Mike Joe grinned, his jaw sagging weakly.

'Lobo Wolf gone,' he said foolishly. 'Lobo Wolf deader'n hell. Mike Joe make'm pay good, yuh dam' right. Tolman, Welden –' Mike Joe lifted his head a little, as though listening. Then he nodded slowly, and began humming a war-song of the Apache, a tuneless sort of a chant. He took a deep breath, and the song was ended.

Sad stepped back against the bar, his eyes filled with sorrow. He could appreciate Mike

Joe's love for his murdered partner and what prompted him to seek revenge. And he had gone out chanting the war-song of his ancestors. Sad unconsciously removed his sombrero, as he looked down at little Mike Joe.

Men were crowding around Sad, asking questions. There was Fairchild, the old doctor, his sleeves rolled to his elbows, the prosecuting attorney, the county clerk, cowboys – all asking questions.

'Yuh must know most of the story,' said Sad wearily. 'If you'll take the JHC connected brand, yuh can fit the Tomahawk right over it. Hawker registered that brand to loot the JHC, after Cleland left here. Frank Welden was in on that deal with Hawker, Ted Bell, Delago, and Heilman. Jones and Simpson were innocent. Then Welden discovered gold on the JHC, and they planned to steal the ranch. Hal Welden wanted his share; so he killed Cleland.

'Tolman advised stealin' the body to prevent Miss Nolan from provin' that Cleland was dead. They got Lobo and Mike to try and steal that will from Miss Nolan, but Lobo got caught, and they killed him to stop his mouth. That was their big mistake, 'cause Lobo was Mike's pardner, and he went out after revenge.'

288

'He stole that shotgun from me,' said Fairchild.

'But there was their big mistake,' said Sad. 'They forged that mortgage, and copied Cleland's name from a letter; a letter that was written and signed by Miss Nolan. They tried in every way to throw the blame on Gavin and his outfit. They kidnaped Miss Nolan and tried to scare her out of the country tonight. They caught Chuck Gavin at the same time, knocked him out and blindfolded him, but I shot his horse, and they left Chuck there, thinking we'd blame Chuck for stealin' her. But it's all cleared up, and the girl gets the JHC – and the gold mine.'

'That is the most amazing story I ever heard,' declared the prosecuting attorney as he followed Sad outside. 'How much of this did you know before Harold Welden made his confession?'

Sad smiled slowly.

'I had to guess at a lot of it. If yo're a wise lawyer, you'll go down to the jail and get a signed confession from Delago right away. Yuh see, Welden never confessed. In fact, he never spoke a word all the way to town.'

The lawyer looked blankly at Sad for several moments.

'Of all the – I'll get that confession right

289

now,' he said and hurried away.

Sad sauntered across the street to the hotel, where he found Chuck and the rest of the J Bar 44 with Clare. Bill Haskell was there, trying to make Bat Gavin understand that it wasn't any fault of his that they had almost hanged Chuck. Swede came in, grinning widely, and did a double-shuffle.

'The money they stole is all in the bank,' he announced. 'Delago said it was in there. Welden was keepin' it for the boys. They destroyed Cleland's body, but Delago swears it was Cleland's body. They're goin' out after Pete Hawker, and that cleans up the gang. There's also fifty thousand worth of bonds in the bank, which belongs to Cleland, so Delago says. My, my, but that boy shore is talkative.'

Elastic Jones and Pima came stumbling in, arguing as usual, but stopped in the doorway and looked at the crowd.

'I'd like to beg yore pardon, Bat,' said Pima slowly. 'I reckon I got the wrong idea all the time, but I'm a man who can back-water any time I find out I'm wrong. Mind shakin' hands with a damned old fool?'

Bat Gavin held out his hand, a grin on his face.

'Same here,' said Elastic. 'I wasn't as rabid as Pima. But I hated you folks a-plenty.'

'I'm glad it's over, Elastic.'

'You was as bad as I was – mebby worse,' said Pima.

Clare came over to Sad, and they looked at each other.

'I am going to get the JHC,' she said softly.

'Shore – that's fine, Clare.'

'And you made it possible, Sad.'

'That's the way it had to work out.'

'I'm going to stay right here; going to be part of the Cinco range. You will stay, won't you – you and Swede? I am going to need good men to run the JHC.'

Sad smiled, looked past her at Chuck, and her eyes followed his gaze. When she turned back, her eyes did not lift above the top button of his stringy old vest.

Sad smiled down at the top of her head as he replied:

'You'll have good men. There'll be water enough for two ranches, and there's that gold mine to develop. Yo're a lucky young woman.'

'And you are the Luck-Maker, Sad.'

'I never thought of that. But we'll be driftin' along soon. We promised Buck Hogan we'd work for him down on the Sweetwater – and this country is kinda tame – now. I'm shore glad to have met you, Clare.'

Clare looked up, her eyes misty with tears.

'But you'll come back some day – and don't forget that I – we – owe everything to you, Sad Sontag.'

'You don't owe nothin' to me – dang it, yuh earned every bit of it. All I ask is that yuh keep Old Pima and Elastic.'

'They stay with me,' quickly. 'I couldn't do without them.'

'That's what I was tellin' Pima,' said Elastic hoarsely. 'He was scared we was out of a job, but I told him that my cookin' and his –'

A man stepped through the doorway, stopped short. It was Grover Harris, the jewelry salesman, as fat and florid as ever, derby hat jolted over one eye, a valise in each hand. He dropped them, shoved his hat back, and started to speak, when his eyes fell upon Clare and Chuck. He blinked foolishly for a moment, picked up his valises and walked out again.

Chuck laughed outright and began to tell his father who Harris was. In the momentary confusion Sad and Swede stepped outside, heading for the jail, where they met the sheriff and the prosecuting attorney.

'I've got that signed confession,' said the lawyer, 'and you boys get the reward money.'

'And I said you was a crazy fool,' reminded

the sheriff. 'Remember that? Well, I take it back. Yo're either dam' smart or awfully lucky.'

'Perhaps,' said the lawyer wisely, 'he is smart enough to make his own luck.'

'I can't tell yuh,' grinned Sad, ' 'cause I ain't smart enough to answer. But I'm goin' to bed, leavin' the door open and my gun on the table. I may not be smart and I may be lucky – but if yuh want to know jist why I did this, I'll tell yuh – it was 'cause I was scared. That train wreck scared me, and I've been scared ever since.'

'Don't tell me that,' grunted the sheriff. 'Scared! Sontag, was you sent in here?'

'Nope.'

'What in hell is yore business?'

'Everybody's.'

'Well,' the sheriff squinted up at the starlit sky and removed his hat, 'thank God for a man who don't specialize.'

In front of the hotel a group of folks were laughing and talking. The yellow light from the Cinco Saloon windows threw highlights on the saddles and backs of the horses at the hitch-rack. Somewhere a phonograph rasped out an old love song, and a dog across the street barked.

Peace had come to Cinco City and the ghost riders were through.